Finding Technicolour

Finding Technicolour

Rebecca Rose

The Peacock Pen
Melbourne

*"Darkness cannot drive out darkness. Only light can do that.
Hate cannot drive out hate. Only love can do that."*

– Martin Luther King

What's the point of painting on a page that is stained?

Chapter ONE

Two weeks ago I almost died. That's what I overheard the doctor tell my mum. Mum sobbed loudly, so I couldn't hear the rest. I gave up eavesdropping. I didn't remember falling back asleep. I did, though, because Mum greeted me with tears and kisses as I woke. Those days I couldn't recall time. The past couple of weeks had been a bit of a blur. A coma will do that to you.

I fell in and out of sleep and didn't know how long I'd been captured in my sleep spells. I'd wake feeling like an amnesiac, but before I could question my circumstance my eyelids weighed me down. I'd fall into what I can only describe as darkness. Pitch black. Almost serenity. I didn't know where I went when I went there, but my body wanted me to go. My mind wanted me to. Sometimes I felt myself crave it. I felt better when I was there. Plus, I didn't like the hospital lights.

I didn't want to see the light.

I opened my eyes and half expected to see Mum gazing over me, her cheeks stained with tears. That's what I'd seen every day for the past week – since I'd been awake. But that day I saw my brother, Liam. He looked at me like it was the last time he'd ever see me, as if a secret goodbye swirled deep within his irises. The skin around his eyes was red, like they'd just been roughly wiped. *Had he been crying?* Our eyes locked. My mind went blank. I didn't know how to feel. His ocean-blue eyes made it seem that I might drown if I looked into them too long. But I continued to stare.

Silent seconds passed. His glimpse of goodbye vanished and a smile stretched across his face. My feeling of drowning expired. I didn't know why, but I was disappointed.

"Hey … Peyton, how you feeling today?"

I wanted to speak, but the lump in my throat got in the way. The words were stuck between my gums and teeth. My mouth felt bone dry. I glanced to my bedside table. My brother grabbed the glass of water and positioned the straw in my mouth. I took several sips then licked my lips. A tingle of pain materialised. It came and went so fast that I ignored it.

I thought about Liam's question, cleared my throat and spoke. "I'm OK …" My voice was hoarse.

I didn't know if I was OK though – isn't that what we say to stop people questioning us further? Isn't that the answer we give so we don't burden others with our troubles? It's what we say to move on to the next thing.

Was I OK? I didn't even know what had happened. *Why had I been in an induced coma?* It had been a little over a week since I'd woken and my question hadn't been answered. When I woke, I'd try to piece things together. Every time I opened my eyes, I'd try to remember something new. I'd lock it away somewhere in my mind and hope the puzzle would become clear.

But it hadn't.

A heavy rush rumbled through my entire body. My mind throbbed. It felt like I was caught in a riptide. I closed my eyes. Forced my lungs to draw deeper.

"P, are you OK?"

Liam's worried words made a stone form in my chest. It weighed heavier with each breath. I don't know how, but I managed to centre myself and ignore the thoughts that made my head spin. My veins pumped with slight relief, but I couldn't shake the feeling that I had done that before. Like forcing myself to neglect – push feelings aside – was something I had done too much of. I let that unfinished recollection trickle to the back of my mind. The panicked rush stole some life out of me. Like a thief it left me feeling weak. I was breathless. Broken.

Tears welled in Liam's eyes. I didn't want that. I couldn't handle that. I tried to warm my voice, make myself sound convincing, so he didn't have to worry. But there he was again, asking me something I was afraid I didn't know the answer to. *Was I OK?*

"Yeah, Liam. I'm fine. Just a little tired."

I saw words form on his tongue. He swallowed them. I knew he knew I was lying. He turned to the sound of the door opening. I watched him as he lifted his hand to wipe away his tears.

My doctor strolled in. He wore the usual white coat you see in the movies and a stethoscope draped around his neck, showcasing his broad shoulders. Not your usual doctor – if there was such a thing. I guess I'd call him handsome. Tanned skin, short mousey-blond hair, emerald eyes and dimples that deepened when he spoke or smiled.

"Good morning, Peyton. Wait, is it still morning?" Dr Handsome checked his watch. "11:56, still morning."

There they were, his dimples, as he smiled at me, trying to lighten the mood. What for, I didn't know. Maybe there was some bad news he wanted to tell me. It would help if I knew what had happened to me in the first place. But I played along and tried to stretch a smile across my face. My skin tightened, almost as if it should have hurt.

Mum entered the room and hurtled towards me. Tears in her eyes. Since I'd been in hospital I was finding it difficult to picture her without tears. She kissed me on the cheek and told me how much she loved me, then took a seat at my bedside.

I scanned the room. Déjà vu. The same three faces had looked upon me when the first bomb was dropped. I remember being told I had just come out of a coma. My heart plummeted. My body no longer felt like it was mine. I saw myself lying in the hospital bed. Hooked up to machines. My long dark hair swept from my face. The rest of the moment was blurred, like a part of my life had been ripped away without my permission. I had been asleep for five days straight. Almost a full week of lying there doing nothing but trying to breathe with the help of machines.

When the words escaped the doctor's mouth, the room was spinning. I couldn't breathe. Memories that weren't mine flooded my brain. My heart pulsed. My bones clattered. My mind wasn't strong enough to hear the rest. Tears streamed down my face. I think I screamed and begged him to stop talking. Stop everything.

After the announcement, I dazed in and out of sleep. Fell in and out of darkness. I didn't want to see the light.

I wasn't ready.

Chapter TWO

I hated being the centre of attention, but there was nothing I could do to divert it. All eyes were on me – each stencilled with worry. I saw the questions smeared over their faces.

"Will she be able to handle it?"

"Is she strong enough to hear the truth?"

I didn't know if I was able to handle it. And after that panic attack, my strength – my energy – was waning. But I wanted to try. I wanted to hear the truth.

I breathed but didn't feel the breath. The oxygen didn't tickle my lungs. I only knew I was breathing because I saw my chest rise and fall. My body felt heavy. Numb. But my mind rushed. *I didn't feel in control.*

It was no longer a want of knowing. It was a need. I needed to know.

"What's going on? What happened to me? Why am I here? I want to leave."

"Sweetheart … Calm down, just let the doctor explain

everything." Mum tried to speak the words soothingly, but her unseen crying made her voice shake.

My sight snapped to Dr Handsome. He clutched a clipboard. In his hands he held the answers I so desperately desired.

"Peyton, as you know you have recently woken up from a five-day induced coma."

As the last few words escaped his lips, the stone in my chest grew heavier. I felt like I couldn't breathe, and I was so numb, I didn't know if I actually was breathing. I tried to push away the panic. I needed to focus my attention on listening. Focus on the truth. I needed to know what had happened.

"There is no easy way to tell you this, but you have been in a car crash."

It took several seconds for my brain to register his words. I found myself mouthing them: car crash.

There it was. The reason I should no longer be on this earth. A tingling sensation took over my limbs, like they were remembering the crash, but the feeling was so faint I almost couldn't feel it. I should have died, yet there I was.

"A car crash? I don't remember that."

"Peyton, you have suffered injuries and a symptom from your harsh head wound can be Post Traumatic Amnesia or PTA."

"Amnesia?"

"Yes. It's where –"

"I *know* what amnesia is."

"P, let the doctor speak …"

I eyed Mum much more harshly than I meant to. She took my bladed stare; her petite body clenched and retreated into the chair. A tear rolled down her cheek. But I couldn't find words for an apology. Not right then. I wanted more answers. *I needed to know.*

I glared at Dr Enderson, who was covered with sympathy. He was calm and collected, confident and concise. I couldn't help but feel jealous of how put-together he was. I knew we were in very different situations, but I could feel myself coming undone.

"I know what amnesia is." I took a breath. "But I don't have that. I don't, because … I still know things. My name, my mum, my brother … Nurses have been asking me those questions. And I did that test over and over, and got stuff right … I, I still remember things."

"That's fantastic, Peyton." Dr Enderson smiled.

I couldn't help but look to his dimples, their sweetness almost soothing.

"Your results on the Westmead PTA scale have been excellent. We still have to continue with tests and treatments to ensure your responsive and conscious states remain at a high level. With everything we have been doing so far, you have responded exceptionally well. I don't doubt that you'll be able to leave the hospital soon and be taking the next step towards your recovery … When you're feeling strong enough, or when you're feeling ready, we can get you into therapy."

I laughed away the thought. "Why would I need therapy?"

"Peyton, you've been through a traumatic event. Attending counselling sessions and speaking to someone outside of your circle will help. You might be able to speak about things that you aren't comfortable talking about with anyone else."

What things? Maybe I did have amnesia. I had no idea what he was speaking about. *Why wouldn't I be able to talk with my family?*

"What happened to me? Do *you* know? Do *any* of you know?" I looked to Mum – her posture had changed. She sat on the edge of the chair and surveyed me like she wished she could trade places.

"It's OK, sweetheart."

"No. It's *not*. I don't remember … I don't remember *any* of it. Was I alone? Was it … was it *my fault?* Did anyone else get *hurt?*"

Mum cupped my hand. She softly stroked my skin, as though at any moment I would break. I glanced down to our hands. My hand. My arm. Bruised. Scratched. Raw. I skipped a breath and retreated from Mum's hold. My arms didn't look like the arms I'd known all of my seventeen years. I touched my face. It didn't feel right. Scabbed. Scrapped. I licked my lips and there it was again, the tingle of pain.

"Mum I … I don't …" A lump locked in my throat. It took a couple of attempts but I swallowed it away. "I don't remember." Tears escaped and ran down my cheeks. I half expected them to sting my skin but could only assume the needle stuck in my arm gave me strong pain relief.

"We know, sweetheart. But it's OK you don't remember just yet."

I saw the rest of her words twist around her tongue. But they wouldn't come out of her mouth. She didn't know what to say, or how to say it. But my mum's words spoken or unspoken wouldn't change the situation. They couldn't.

"Was it my fault? Did anyone else get hurt? *Please* just tell me … I *need* to know."

"From what we know, Peyton, it was only you in the crash," Dr Enderson said.

I locked my sight to the ceiling, relieved. But a sudden haunted feeling struck – I still didn't know what had happened. I didn't know the truth.

Chapter THREE

I didn't really remember the passing days. Only fragments. I didn't know if that was because of my supposed Post Traumatic Amnesia or because I had become somewhat skilled at repressing thoughts. Feelings. Memories.

I was moved from one part of the hospital to another. I read the words 'Rehab Facility' as I was wheeled to my new room. I didn't soak in my surroundings. The walls were just walls. The sanitised stench didn't clear my sinuses. The nurses' and patients' faces were just a blur – blank canvases I had no interest in detailing. I didn't lock onto the sound of echoed voices and footsteps or feel the need to unravel their stories, knowing that that would only remind me of how much I didn't want to be there.

Being told about the crash and truly acknowledging my injuries made me zone out. It allowed me to hide in my darkness, a place where I didn't have to think.

I didn't have to see the light.

While I was being checked I remembered certain moments. My results suggested everything was fine. I was doing fine. For another week I underwent physical therapy to ensure I could walk, talk and operate my body without difficulties. I was lucky my motor skills weren't affected. I could do everything. I was a little shaky. My hands trembled whenever I used them. But I was told the more I used them and continued the exercises, the stronger they'd become. Internally, I was recovering quickly. It had been over four weeks since the crash and my body had recovered quicker than the doctor predicted. He was very pleased with my improvements. Externally, I would heal. I would have scars. My skin would be forever bound with the marks of the accident. The crash I didn't remember. I didn't know if I wanted that. *Could the scars be beautiful?* But I was alive. *I think that's what I wanted.* It was most certainly what my mum and my brother wanted. They had been at the hospital and rehab facility with me every day. I don't know what I would do without them.

The doctor said I was going to be OK, and if everything went as predicted, I would be able to go home in a few days. But at that time, even though I didn't want to be there, the thought of being OK didn't feel like enough, especially to go home. To go back to reality. Every time a nurse came to take me to the room for tests, I'd dread it. It was a waste of time. I watched as the hands turned on the clock. I'd count the dragging minutes until I could go back to my room. Back to sleep. Back to the dark.

It was night. The dull bedside lamp cloaked the room. I was alone with Mum. Other than the humming of some electric device, we were wrapped in silence. I didn't know what to say to free us from the quiet.

"Peyton."

My muscles froze. I knew what she was about to ask. I didn't want her to, but I didn't have the strength or a valid reason to stop her.

"Why did you go driving by yourself? You knew I was finishing work in an hour. We could have gone and done some night driving when I got home ... Why didn't you wait?"

I didn't look at her, but I knew she was perched at the edge of the chair. I felt her stare. Even through this morphine numbness I felt the sting of her eyes.

"I don't remember." I wasn't lying. But a heavy feeling weighed me down, making me believe that I would remember the truth soon. And now I wasn't sure if I wanted to.

My head rested on the pillow as I stared at the stains on the wall. I wondered whether if I didn't blink then maybe I'd get to see them expand. My dedication was disrupted when Mum and Liam strolled in.

"Oh you're awake. Morning, sweetheart. How are you feeling today?" Mum gently kissed my forehead.

I was sick of that question. My status hadn't changed. I was stuck in an unfamiliar mind and a room I didn't want to be in. My eyes answered for me.

Mum softly grinned and placed herself on a chair. "P, what I'm about to say might surprise you, but there's no need to panic or worry …"

"What?"

"The police are coming to speak with you today."

I set my wide eyes on Liam. His features showed concern but quickly glazed with reassurance. "It'll be all right, P," he said. "They're just going to ask you about the crash."

Two officers stepped into the room. The man was tall with big eyes, his skin like melted chocolate. The woman was short and appeared even more petite because of her partner's height. Her thick dark fringe dominated her forehead and enforced her light complexion. They stood at the end of my bed. Their uniforms identical. The fluorescent vests made me uncomfortable – it was a colour I wasn't ready to see. Knowing that it would draw attention, I didn't squint or close my eyes. Their presence made me crave my darkness and, even though I'd just woken up, I was willing to force myself back into the shadows.

"Hello Peyton, I'm Officer Kole and this is my partner Officer Lacy. We're here today to ask you a couple of questions about your accident."

Mum, Liam and I listened to the police and answered what we could. I decided to use my diagnosis to my advantage and told them I couldn't remember much. It was the truth, but something inside made me feel like it was a lie. Like there was something I could do to make myself remember.

It was when we were advised to seek a lawyer that I realised how serious this was becoming. I was worried for the result. Worried about what would happen to me. I knew driving without a licence was reckless, but I remember feeling that I had to – that I had no other choice.

Time doesn't fly when you're cooped up in a rehab room and your daily routine is the same – almost by the second. But somehow the day came for me to go home. I guessed, for the doctors, my status had changed to 'OK'. Mum and Liam were ready to take me. *I guess it was really happening.*

I had no regrets at leaving the unflattering hospital gown behind me. For the first time in what felt like forever, I was dressed in my clothes. A jumper and jeans. Even though I could walk and operate my body without difficulty, I slumped in a wheelchair, embarrassed, as I was slowly trundled out to the carpark. A part of me was nervous about getting into the car, but I wasn't going to let that bubble to the surface. I was finally being freed from a place I didn't want to be. But my reality almost didn't feel real to me.

The drive was dull. The radio low. Mum drove slowly so all the cars overtook us. She said she wanted me to feel safe. I wanted to tell her to put her foot on the pedal and just get me home. Instead I smiled and thanked her. I really was happy she cared about me so much.

I stared out the window. Winter was upon us. Everywhere

looked grey. The clouds. Trees. Roads. The drizzling rain. I was glad the world looked like that. I don't think I could've coped any other way.

I wasn't ready for colour.

I made my way to the kitchen table, following Mum's kind-hearted orders. She said she wanted to make us all lunch and that the three of us were going to have our first family meal since my return home. But I knew the real reason we were doing it.

Thick slabs of bread were stacked in front of us, with whatever filling Mum could find in the fridge. I smiled. I had missed the two of them – even though they were at my bedside every day since the crash. My heart missed the small moments that now seemed so rare.

I wasn't hungry, but I took a couple of bites to show Mum I was trying. I knew what was about to happen and I wished she would start it already. Liam devoured his sandwich and Mum ate half of hers before she said what she really planned the lunch for. She looked to my brother. Then both of their eyes set on me. *Had they planned the speech? Were they going to tag-team on me?*

Mum grinned. "P, I want us to talk about your therapy sessions."

"Mum, I'm *not* doing them."

"P, just listen to what Mum has to say," Liam said.

I knew he cared. I knew they both cared, but I didn't

want to speak with a stranger. It just didn't sit right with me. I didn't believe that going to therapy was something that would help. There was nothing wrong with me. Well, nothing that words would fix.

"I don't want to talk with a therapist."

"But Dr Enderson said …"

"I don't *care* what he …"

"Well Peyton, *I* do." Mum's words escaped firmly but her body and face retracted the meanness they were soaked in. She must've felt sorry for me. "*Please* P, just entertain the idea. Go a couple of times. Just try it for a couple of sessions. You never know, it might help …"

I couldn't fight her on that request. Any other time pre-accident I would've been able to slither my way out of it. Convince her it was unessential. But I saw the pain in her eyes. I didn't want her to worry any more. I wanted to make her happy.

"OK. I'll go. I'll try it."

Chapter FOUR

I had two days to convince Mum I didn't need to go through with the therapy sessions. Two days to show her and Liam that they weren't needed. But I couldn't do it. Instead I wasted the forty-eight hours. Remembering the reasons why I had convinced myself to agree to them in the first place – I wanted to show Mum I was OK, I wanted Liam to step off a little more. I hoped that if I went to therapy they'd give me room to breathe. I left the topic alone. We all did, knowing it would only cause unwanted tension.

I got in the car with Mum. That day, she drove a little faster. Bicycles couldn't overtake us. We drove down our long windy street. The similar brick houses on either side of the street always looked bland in winter. My eyes stretched over the footpath that led to an oval where kids played cricket and football. We rolled to traffic lights exiting our middle-class suburb and headed towards town, where the large shopping centre and restaurants were. We lived about fifty minutes away from the city and about forty-five minutes from what I describe as secluded country – houses surrounded by empty paddocks wrapped with the stench of manure and the closest neighbour was miles away. As Mum and I made our way to the designated address through the busying streets of town, I glanced out the rain-soaked window, ignoring the pedestrians. My fondness of people and discovering their stories was fading. The rain scurried down the windows and I wondered if from the outside it looked like I was crying. The dark clouds hung overhead. The world was still grey. I was thankful, because when my eyes were open, I could pretend I was still in my darkness.

We pulled up to a chunky brown-brick building. It looked uninviting. Mum parked the car then at looked me. I watched as she carefully chose her words. I knew she wasn't going to say exactly what she wanted. She took a breath. "Peyton, thank you for trying this." She smiled at me. But it was weak.

I knew she was preparing herself for me to argue with her. Tell her I didn't want the stupid sessions. That I didn't want to speak with a stranger. I looked at her face. For the first time in what felt like forever, her cheeks weren't stained with tears, but I could tell her ducts were working overtime to stall them. I swallowed my want to protest. "Bye Mum." I left the car and slowly stepped towards the next hour of my life.

A car horn sounded. I slapped my hand over my mouth to conceal a scream as I searched the almost empty carpark. The noise wasn't directed at me, just some idiot driver over the road. Still, my body trembled like a leaf in a winter breeze. I looked to Mum. She had launched out of the car, left the door open and was jogging towards me.

"I'm OK!" I waved her away and hoped I convinced her I was alright.

She nodded as she slid backwards, clutching on to the car door. I felt her stare as I continued forward. She wanted to come in with me; not into the session, but to sign in and wait with me. We negotiated but I found myself getting what I wanted. I told her that I agreed to go to therapy if she just dropped me off. I think she let me have what I wanted because all *she* wanted was for me to follow the doctor's advice. I knew she would sit in the car, waiting in the car park for me and if I were ever to come to another therapy session, I predicted she would hang about and spend the hour in a café. I saw her quickly scanning the area.

I drew a deep breath, pushed the door open and stepped to the reception desk. A blond-haired woman perched behind it, her hair tied tightly in a large bun with every strand off her face. Her makeup was light and complimented her natural beauty. She was in her mid to late twenties, dressed in a cream blouse, corporate yet casual. Everything about her seemed perfect and kind of made me dislike her. There I was, a crumpled mess with visible injuries, about to speak with a model. I cleared my throat, wanting to get it over with.

"Hi, my name's Peyton Swift. I have an appointment here today."

Her large brown eyes lit. "Hi Peyton. Dr Wilson will be right with you. Just make yourself comfortable in the waiting area." She smiled. And there it was, the final thing that made me have to hate her. Two perfectly straight rows of white teeth. I smiled the most politely I could, then made my way to the waiting area.

The room was bright. Clean. Shapely cushioned furniture surrounded a glass coffee table. Newspapers and glossy magazines were neatly organised. For some reason I felt like I was placed in a catalogue advertisement; all that was missing was a flat-screen TV on the wall and a large dog curled up on a soft rug. The ugly outside bricks had been deceiving.

"Miss Swift?"

A tall man stood in the hallway, dressed in a light-blue long-sleeve shirt and black trousers.

"Hello," he smiled. "I'm Greg Wilson. Please come this way …" He stuck out his hand like he expected me to follow him in an eccentric dance. I plodded to where his whole hand directed and entered the room. It was clean, with a subtle floral aroma. The neutral tones were colours I wasn't ready for. But I had to keep my eyes open. I couldn't unveil my weakness. Furniture was positioned just so. Everything appeared in its place. Pens and papers were arranged on his desk. Waiting there to take notes on me – analyse my thoughts.

"Please take a seat."

I chose a cream chair at his desk and slumped into faux comfort, my arms crossed over my torso. My eyes strained over the papers. I hoped to read some answers or discover something new about the crash. But they were blank.

Dr Wilson settled in his chair on the other side of the table. His ankle rested on his knee. His short hair and beard were dark grey. The musky aroma of his aftershave sat in my nostrils. I liked the smell and breathed in deeply, trying to catch as much as I could before he questioned my breathing style. Quickly I moved on to the next thing to look at and caught his eyes. Long dark lashes bordered light-grey irises, encompassed with flecks of blue as the light hit them. They were magical. I'd never seen anything like them.

He observed me kindly. Let me become familiar with my whereabouts. He probably believed I would be visiting him every week for at least three months, like Dr Enderson had prescribed. But Dr Wilson was wrong. I would only be seeing him for two weeks. Two sessions to prove to Mum that I tried it out but it wasn't for me.

"How are you Miss Swift?"

"Just call me Peyton."

"Oh, OK … How are you today, Peyton?"

"Shouldn't I be lying down to answer these questions?"

"If that's what you want. Whatever makes you comfortable."

I remained still.

"So Peyton, have you ever been to a therapy session before? Or had any experience with counselling?"

"No."

"I can tell you're a little apprehensive about this entire thing. Can I say a little *peeved* that you have to be here? From my many years of experience I must admit that sometimes it's easier for patients to open up when they willingly book sessions, but when they're admitted, it's a little different … I *do* know that when they open up, they feel better. They even tell me so. And it *does* become easier as we progress. The fact that you're here sitting in this room is a huge step."

My stare at him felt harsh, but I couldn't undo it now.

"Is there anything you want to discuss today?" He looked at me softly – kind, waiting for a response.

I didn't have one.

"This hour is all yours. Whatever you want to talk about." His voice was warm. I couldn't help wanting him to speak again, just so I could hear it. I thought he had the perfect voice for audio books. "Let me remind you that this is all confidential. Nothing you say will leave this room."

I inspected the neutral area. Framed certificates hung on the wall. A jar full of water and two small glasses on a small round table. A box of tissues on another. As I continued to analyse the space, I was reminded that I didn't want to be there. I didn't need to be there. He couldn't fix my vulnerabilities through his bachelor-degree spoken words.

"What do you already know about me?"

I saw Dr Wilson's eyes study me. He was surprised. I assumed it wasn't a question he heard regularly.

"Come on, you *must* know something. I was given to you *specifically* by Dr Enderson. You *have* to know something."

"Peyton, all I know is that you were in some sort of accident. What you tell me about it is up to you. What you want to share with me, is all up to you."

"Well, Dr Enderson must have told you that these therapy sessions are something I *didn't* agree to doing, nor something I *want* to do or have any interest in … So don't expect to get much from me."

The minutes slowly ticked away. We small talked. I gave him nothing. *Why would I share with a perfect stranger? What was I meant to be sharing? How could I speak with someone I didn't know, someone I didn't trust? Why go to therapy and speak about a crash I didn't even remember?*

Speaking to him wasn't going to change my past.

Any of it.

Chapter FIVE

I woke in a rush of sweat from the nightmares I couldn't remember. I tossed the blankets off my injured body and showered, letting the hot steam comfort me as the water soaked my scabs. Some had left my body, leaving me with fresh pink skin. Others would become scars. *Would they be beautiful?*

I turned the taps off and let the water descend, then stood still until my naked body was cold and covered in goose bumps. I grabbed the towel and wrapped it around me. Warmth slowly spread over my skin. For a split second I felt OK.

It had almost been a week since my first therapy session and I was dreading my return to that place. Nothing had changed since I'd been there. There was nothing new I remembered. In the one week and two days since I had been home, Mum had tiptoed around the house making sure things were fine –

that I was fine. I was. I think. At least that's what I wanted her to think. I didn't want her to be any more concerned than she had been.

I knew she was stressing about the police and the charges that I might be facing. She tried to hide her worries, but I caught her sitting on the floor counting the coins she had in her secret money jar. I was worried about the charges too. I was stupid not to think about the consequences. I was stupid to think I could drive with just my learner's permit, alone in the dark. But this gut feeling swivelled in my insides reminding me I hadn't had a choice.

Since being home I still felt like a patient. I knew I'd feel better if Mum stopped being so gentle. There might be some normalcy back in my life if she stopped making me feel smothered.

Liam had gone back to college. I convinced myself that I wasn't sad to say goodbye; I knew that's where he needed to be. Not at home with me. He had already taken too many weeks off to stay at my bedside and make sure Mum was stable. I remembered lying in the hospital bed telling him to go back to college, telling him I was OK, that Mum and I were going to be OK, that it was alright for him to go.

Although I love my brother to death, a part of me was relieved that he'd left. I didn't need two people tiptoeing around me. He sent me a couple of text messages, which made me miss him.

Liam: Just arrived back on campus … This place is crazy

P! Promise me u won't tell mum what happened the other week. Almost being expelled would've been the beginning of the end.

Me: I promise I won't. My lips r sealed big brother. But I expect to reap rewards 4 my silence!

Liam: & u shall baby sister. Ask & if it's in my power it shall be yours.

Me: OK. Speak soon then. And Liam try to stay out of trouble! X

Liam: Speak soon. Miss u P! xx

During my early recovery Mum shortened her hours at work, but the lack of money began to take its toll. It took me a few days, but I convinced her to go back to working her usual hours, in turn giving me much-needed free time. Time to think. Maybe even time to remember the crash.

I've gone hours without remembering something, but days without remembering is like torture. And a part of me wasn't even sure I wanted to remember the whole truth.

The days slithered by and I still couldn't recall the accident. When it happened. Why. How it happened. Trying to remember it was like trying to remember a stranger's memory. Every time I tried to think about it, a haunting feeling took over. Each time the feeling darkened then flashes of memories sparked. I shook them away before they became too real. Before they became too clear. Before I knew what they were and I had to remember.

I knew I was blocking something. A little bit of me

remembered what it was. But I didn't want it to be real. It couldn't be real. That's why I shook them away. Maybe even why I craved my dark place.

At the second therapy session I sank into the same cream chair with my legs crossed. Dr Wilson's magical grey eyes focused on me. *I wondered if I stared into them for a certain amount of time, would they hypnotise me to speak my darkest secrets?* I looked away before he had the chance to try.

"Peyton, how are you feeling today?"

"I'm OK." *Let's move onto the next thing shall we?* Who was I kidding? I knew it didn't work like that in therapy.

"You know this hour is for you and if you choose not to talk, that's up to you. But I'm here to listen. I'm here to help."

I sighed. He didn't know, but this would be our last session together. I knew I had to say something, just in case Dr Enderson or Mum asked if I had given it my best shot. So I decided to talk about the reason why I was there in the first place.

"A little while ago I was in a car crash, but I don't remember the accident."

"And how does that make you feel?"

"*Really?*" The word wasn't supposed to leave my mind. "Sorry, I just ..."

"It's fine ... When you're ready."

"I actually don't remember certain days leading up to the crash either, and I don't like not knowing ... I was in an induced coma for five days and I feel like a part of my life, a part of my story, has been stolen. Those days feel like chapters or paragraphs unwritten. Not that I'm a writer, more of a painter and drawer."

"An artist; that's interesting."

"I haven't drawn or painted in a while."

"Why is that?"

"Because things with school got in the way."

"Well what did you like to paint?"

"Anything really. You could put a paint brush in my hand and I'd paint what I imagined or what I could see right in front of me."

"Do you think you'll paint again?"

"What, now that I've dropped out of school?"

"When did you drop out of school?"

Wow. Nobody had told him anything. "A few months ago, much to my mum's disapproval."

"Did you not want to continue with your studies?"

There they were again. Those flash memories. I shook them from my head.

"I don't want to talk about it." I leapt from my seat and continued to shake my head, hoping the imagery didn't find a fresh place to latch onto, that it would just seep to the back of my mind.

"Peyton, are you OK?"

I didn't answer. I focused on ignoring the flashes. I had done that before. I could do that again. "I think I want to finish for today."

Chapter SIX

Again, I awoke in a rush of sweat. Still I couldn't remember the nightmares. I was relieved that I still had safety in darkness. Maybe not remembering was for the best. As I showered I picked at my wet scabs, the ones just beginning to come away from my skin. I knew I shouldn't, but I couldn't help myself. *I liked the pain.* I ripped one off. The sting swelled as the hot water hit it. The blood trickled down my arm, descending with the water to become nothing. It made its way down the drain like it was never mine.

After being home for two weeks I still felt like a broken puzzle. There was a piece missing but I didn't know if I was ready to find it.

I took the pain medication I'd been prescribed and, as Doctor Handsome had ordered, I went for a walk. I wrapped myself in layers covering my scabs and scarring. The injuries scattered across my legs, shoulders, arms and face. They were healing well, but their decreasing presence worried me – I wanted them there.

My long dark hair was tied in a ponytail. It blew wildly in the winter wind as I walked along the damp pavement, left with my own thoughts. I began to panic. Worried that the memory flashes would begin again. I focused on stepping over the cracks. Focused everything on not wanting to fall through the pavement.

It was a twelve-minute walk to the local shops. I knew, because I timed how long I could last in the outside world. How long I could last around other people.

The stopwatch continued.

I made my way to the coffee shop – the one Liam and I would always go to when we wanted to talk about life. It was the place he told me about his plan to get his sleeve tattoo two days after his eighteenth birthday – to what would be our mum's short-lived disapproval. It had been over a year and I knew she liked it. The coffee shop was the place where I told him I wanted to travel the world and create art forever. Since Liam's been at college, I haven't been in. It didn't feel right without him. But this was where my feet walked me. And being there helped me almost imagine he was there too. It wouldn't be as much fun, but I had to get out there. Keep living.

The bell rang above the door. My nose was attacked by the strong smell of coffee. The place was fairly empty – a few customers scattered around the small tables. I looked at the stopwatch: fourteen minutes and twenty-two seconds in the outside. The count continued.

Peering around the room, I knew a larger crowd would

have made me abort my outing. I made my way to the counter and ordered an iced coffee.

I hid at a corner table, as far away from people as I could, and scanned the walls bursting with colour. A part of me was unprepared, but my inner artist was tempted to be awed. New original painted canvases hung around the place. I had always dreamt of them showing a piece of my art on their walls, but I was always too scared to ask how I could get it up there. One time Liam was going to ask for me, but I begged him not to. Told him my pieces weren't ready for public display. I knew he didn't believe me because he'd seen my work and told me how amazing it was, but he didn't ask the manager. Now the thought of having my artwork displayed there felt like a distant dream. A little girl's wish.

My eyes continued to search the room. Every chair and table was different. Mismatched. But somehow it worked. Everything complimented. Balanced. The coffee shop hadn't changed that much since Liam and I were last there, even though it felt like decades ago. Unexpected happiness drove through my veins, making me acknowledge that not everything had to change. And maybe I could actually be OK.

A young guy with light brown hair, which looked like a mop on top of his head, came smiling towards me. I didn't know what to do with myself. I tugged at my sleeves as my heart raced. My eyes travelled down his lean body dressed in black from head to toe, to see him holding my drink order. I sighed. My nerves abandoned me.

"Here's your iced coffee. Was there anything else?"

He looked right into my eyes. I couldn't help but stare. His right eye was blue and his left was brown. The soft curls of his hair shaped his tanned face. He smiled at me, his lips stretched across his cheeks.

"No that's it. Thanks."

"I hope you don't mind me asking, but what happened?" He gestured across his cheek and lips.

I assumed he thought asking '*What happened to your face?*' was a little harsh. For some reason, I honestly never expected to be questioned about my appearance. My injuries. I hadn't prepared myself for a moment like this.

He beamed as he waited for a response. A bright picture framed with intrigue.

I wasn't in the mood to share with an outsider and hoped our conversation would be over before it began. So I tried to make my answer simple. Short. "It's just a couple of scratches."

"Ah … So they're your wounds from battle?"

I didn't respond.

"What does the other person look like?"

The car? Words left my lips before I gave them permission. "Completely crushed. Shattered even."

That's what Mum told me. The old banger of a car was unfixable. Much to Liam's despair, I imagined. He would never admit losing the car broke his heart a little, but I knew how much he loved it. I felt guilty for ruining it. I lost count of the hours he and his friends spent on fixing it, making it roadworthy. I won't forget the times I helped him with it too. The lessons he gave me about cars and engines. Even though most of the terminology went over my head and what he taught me never really sank in, spending time together was enough for me. The ways he'd get me to laugh. And how we recited our favourite lines from our favourite movies. And when we blasted the radio and sang at the top of our lungs. I won't forget that. It's what I hold dear. They're the moments I want to remember.

Before I knew it the coffee-shop guy had plonked himself across from me, swivelled a chair and was leaning back. At first I was reluctant to talk, but our conversation almost felt natural. I don't remember what he said, but he got me to laugh. Something I thought my body had forgotten to do.

After a while an unexpected silence travelled between us. It probably lasted for only several seconds but it was several seconds too long. He grinned at me cheekily.

"Well, I better get back to work. Nice to meet you, err … We didn't properly introduce ourselves, the name's Kai Pearson. And you are?"

"I'm Peyton."

"Peyton?"

"Swift."

"Well Peyton Swift, it's a pleasure to meet you."

"Uh, you too. Bye."

Before more words could be exchanged, I fled the shop, sprinting down the pavement almost tripping over my feet. *I wasn't a runner.* I looked to the stopwatch – two hours, thirty-three minutes and fourteen seconds. Time does fly when you're having fun. He did get me to laugh.

Chapter SEVEN

Mum had the day off. She wanted to spend time with me. So she came up with the idea to go shopping and grab coffee. A girls day. I went along with the idea. I loved my mum. I'd do anything for her. God knows how much she's done for Liam and me. But I wasn't in the mood to shop. Even before the accident it was never one of my favourite things to do. But it was a day to hang out – just the two of us. I didn't really care what we were doing, as long as we were together. I had survived a car accident that should have killed me. I shouldn't have been complaining about the luxury to shop. I was alive. *I think that's what I wanted.*

They say "Shop till you drop" and we did. Even though I kindly declined – several times – Mum insisted on the splurge. She bought me a new pair of jeans and a few winter jumpers. They were dark, big and baggy. The way I wanted them. Easier to hide. Mum tried to shove some colour into the pile, but I wasn't ready. I wanted to be surrounded only by things that took me to my dark place. A place I felt comfortable. A place I still found myself craving.

On the drive home, Mum said she had a place in mind for us to get something to eat and drink. Even though my appetite was still minimal, I agreed. I wanted to continue hanging out. For the entire day, she had been so comfortable with me. The most she'd been since I'd been home. There were still moments when she treated me like a feather, but I overlooked them.

She was a young mum. She had Liam when she was nineteen, and me a couple of years later. I couldn't imagine my brother being a dad. He was so irresponsible. She had sacrificed so much for us to be where we were. We're not the richest people, or the poorest. We have what we need and usually don't ask for more.

I could tell Mum was getting used to driving at a normal pace with me in the car. We almost matched other car speeds. She drove just under the limit, but I could tell she was driving with extra caution. She didn't know this, but a couple of times I watched her reverse down the driveway, then speed down the road as she made her way to work. Secretly I just wanted her to act like she did before. I didn't want her to change. I didn't want her walking on eggshells when she was around me. She used to call drivers "Assholes" or "Scumbags" when they'd cut her off or drive ill mannered. She rarely said something like that now. I felt like she stopped saying stuff like that to protect me. As if her driver's tongue would trigger me into my darkness or a panicked state. But I wanted things to go back to normal. I wanted to feel normal again.

I waited for a driver to cut in front of us, or do something stupid for me to shout at them "Douchebag". But cuss words never felt natural leaving my lips. Mum always laughed at my failed attempts. She was glad her sometimes-vile tongue didn't get passed down to me. Liam inherited it. The only time I used bad language was when I was angry – really angry. Other than that, it just wasn't me.

I gave up waiting for the opportunity to reignite Mum's driver's tongue. Instead I gazed at her as we continued our pleasant drive. We have the same blue eyes and heart-shaped face, but she seemed to pull everything off better than me. Her face has light wrinkles and I felt guilty for bringing them out. When she smiled at me, I felt warm and safe. I always loved that about her when I was kid. But now a heavy feeling weighed my stomach because I knew I was keeping a secret from her. I pushed the feeling aside as best I could and continued to admire her natural beauty. She said if she had the money she'd go under the knife, but I told her I'd protest and slap the knife from the surgeon's hand if it came to that. She had one hand on the wheel and with the other she tucked her light brown hair behind her ear. It waved down just past her shoulders. I smiled. *I love you Mum.*

When we pulled into the local shops, my jaw dropped. "Where are we eating?"

"Here." She smiled. "I know how much you and Liam like coming here. And the three of us used to come here quite a bit when you were younger. I haven't been here in ages, so I thought it might be nice if we did."

I also hadn't been in there in ages. Now there I was again – the next day. *I hoped Kai wasn't there.*

Mum and I strolled in. The bell rang overhead and there he was on the other side of the room, dressed all in black, just like the day we met. He gave this small group of girls their orders. They giggled – he must have said something funny. *Was it the same thing he had said to me?* Not that I remembered what it was. Kai turned around, an empty tray under his arm. Our eyes met. A large smile stretched across his face. I immediately looked away. Mum was looking at the menu board. She linked our arms then led us to an empty table, where we set down.

"Mum. I think we should …"

"Hello again Peyton Swift," Kai said.

Mum glanced to him and then at me. She grinned.

This was not what she thought. *This was not happening.*

"Hey," I said.

"Just come up to the counter when you're both ready to order." Kai moseyed off.

Mum leant over the table to me and whispered a little too loudly. "He's nice. When did you meet him?"

I snapped around and hoped he hadn't heard. Kai was nowhere to be seen. I assumed he was somewhere in the back room.

"I told you, yesterday I went for a walk."

"You didn't tell me about *him*."

"Mum."

"What? Don't you think he's cute? *I* do."

"Mum … There's more about a person then their physical appearance."

Kai *was* cute. I wasn't going to take that away from him. But I didn't know him. I had known of him for less than twenty-four hours. I didn't know how I was supposed to feel about him.

Mum and I ate our food. For a little while we leant back in the chairs, allowing digestion to take its course as we discussed plot theories for one of our favourite TV shows. We looked at the time and decided to make our way back home. *Finally.*

Kai approached us. "How was the food? Was it that bad you're leaving already?"

Mum liked his joke. She giggled. "No, the food was delicious. Thank you. We really enjoyed it."

He looked to me. His blue/brown irises searched my face as if he were seeking another truth. An answer to a question he hadn't asked yet.

"Yeah." I nodded and rushed a smile. "The food was great. But we better get going."

"Hang out with me."

"What? *When?*" The second question wasn't supposed to slip through my lips.

"Right now."

"Oh, um, sorry. I've gotta go with Mum."

"No Peyton, you don't. You can go …"

Why Mum? Why?

"Are you up for it then?" Kai asked.

"Yes she is." I glared at her. A bright smile stretched across her face. She leant in, kissed me on the cheek and hugged me. She whispered in my ear. "You've got to get back out there." She kissed my cheek again, then left without another glance back.

I looked at Kai. He smiled proudly like he had just accomplished something.

Chapter EIGHT

I was left alone. Caught in the shop. Kai told me not to move as he went to the back and signed off for the day. As I stood by myself I prepared my escape, but every direction I thought to take resulted in him running after me or catching up with me too easily. I wasn't a runner – pre- or post-accident.

"Ready?"

I turned around. Kai appeared behind me – a little too close for my liking. He wore a black leather jacket and looked like a gothic surfer. Yet somehow it made him look cooler. I awkwardly twirled, pushed the door open – pushing away the unwanted thoughts of him and me from my mind – then stepped outside. The fresh air whipped my cheeks and the cold stung my lungs. Everything was decorated in grey. Or was that the way I painted it? Either way it didn't matter. It was the way I wanted it be – the way I wanted it to look.

"So, where do you wanna go for you to 'get back out there'?" Kai said.

"You heard *that*?"

"Your mum's not the quietest whisperer …"

My heart sank. I hoped he hadn't heard her earlier *whispering*. I looked away, embarrassed. *What was I even doing here?*

"So what's your story?" Kai said.

"Excuse me?"

"What's your deal? First you lie to me about how you got your injuries. Then you try to ditch me and use your mum as an excuse. If you didn't want to hang out all you had to do was say."

My eyes widened. He was bluntly honest. And somehow he seemed to read me like a book he'd read a thousand times. I was twisting with conflicting emotions. My stomach turned. I didn't like the way he'd just made me feel. "No … I …"

"So you *do* wanna hang out?"

There it was again, that smug smile – like he'd forced me to admit something.

"I don't know. Maybe."

"Well, all right then." I watched him light up like a bulb. "I know a cool place in the forest we can hang out at. I go there myself just to think. And the scenery is spectacular."

My bones began to clatter. I felt the blood rush through my veins. For seconds my surroundings spun. *I wanted my darkness.* I looked to Kai's eyes. They were bright headlights. I felt my guard rise.

"Um, no thanks. I'm not going to any secluded area for you to kill me. I've already escaped death this year. I'm not game for a second round."

"Interesting. Your plot thickens. And my curiosity increases. Is that how you got your injuries?"

"That's for me to know–"

"And for me to find out. I accept the challenge."

"It's *not* a challenge."

"Fine. Whatever you say. Maybe one day you'll tell me. Maybe you won't. But I'm hoping you will."

Incredible. Unbelievable actually. There he was again, thinking he could knock down my walls and peak inside, then ditch me and leave me lonely. He swept his hand through his thick hair and I couldn't help but feel like I was supposed to be falling for him. Like that was a move he would use to charm other girls. But I wasn't going to allow myself to fall.

We strolled around the corner then stopped in front of a jet-black motorbike, which would have shone if the sun were hitting it. Instead, the day was grey and smelt like it was about to rain. I glanced at him, dressed in his leather jacket, and put two and two together.

"Is this yours?"

"Sure is. Hop on."

"Um. No."

"Have you never been on a motorbike?" Kai asked.

I shook my head.

"Are you *serious*?"

I just eyed him.

"You'll be fine. I'll take it slow. Trust me."

Trust him. I barely knew him and he wanted me to trust

him. *Who was this kid?* There was no way I was getting on that thing. I had just survived a car crash – I was supposed to be scared to get in a car and for some odd reason I wasn't. But clinging onto a stranger on the back of a motorbike was another thing entirely.

"Are we going for a ride on this thing?" Kai said.

"No. Not today."

There it was again, that smug smile. *What was he thinking this time?*

"Good to know," Kai said.

"Good to know *what?*"

"Well, you said 'Not today'. That means we'll be seeing each other again. Hanging out again. Thus allowing me to convince you to take a chance on the motorbike and maybe on me."

He was full of himself. That cheeky smile stretched across his face and his eyes lit up like a hundred different things were running through his mind. A part of me wanted to know more about him. There was no denying he was interesting. I felt myself becoming somewhat captivated, even though I tried to fight it. I wanted to push the secrets out of him. I wanted to hear his story. To understand his *deal*. I also wanted to walk away and have nothing to do with him. Just leave it as the odd chance meeting and in time slowly forget about him. Liam and I would just have to find another favourite café.

My mind rustled up words as I tried to create an excuse for my departure. I latched onto one, but before I could speak, Kai spoke.

"OK, so no motorbike today. No forest exploring today. How about that picnic table over there ..." He pointed. My eyes followed his fingers. "Completely out in the open. People on the road can see us; people in the shops can see us. Too many witnesses for any crime to take place. What do you think?"

I don't remember agreeing, but the next thing I realised we were occupying the table.

Chapter NINE

The smell of rain grew stronger, but nothing fell from the clouds. A fresh wind clutched at my cheeks and my body trembled. Kai and I sat opposite each other. I focused everywhere but his eyes. I didn't want him to read me again.

"Tell me something," Kai said.

"What?"

"Tell me something about you … something I don't already know."

I gave up and looked at him. "You don't know me at all."

"That makes it easier for you then." Kai gazed at me. Like he was discovering some form of hidden treasure.

I decided to be honest. "I don't like strangers."

"Well I'm glad we're not strangers then."

I scrunched my face. *I was pretty sure we were.*

"We met yesterday, so that makes us acquaintances."

Smart-ass. Even in silence my cursing felt offbeat. But it was my first thought. "Tell me something about *you* then."

"I like all things new. New people. New stories. New adventures."

"Your life must be pretty exciting."

"It is. It's even better now you're in it."

Did he really just say that?

"How did you know that I lied about my injuries?"

"Hey, it's my turn to ask you something."

I just glared at him. Waited for an answer.

"But I'll bend the rules for you." He smiled. "Well, I wasn't a hundred per cent sure, but now that you've admitted it, I am … I know what fighting injuries look like, bruises, cuts and all. I've had a few myself. And the injuries you have, they're not from that type of fight."

I didn't like that he knew so much about me just from looking at me. Vulnerable was an emotion I was tired of feeling.

"Tell me something else. What's something you love, or like to do?" Kai said.

I didn't want to tell him anything else. I felt like he already knew too much. But words slipped from my lips. "Um, I like painting,"

"Cool. What do you paint?"

"Whatever I feel like. It doesn't matter."

"Even cooler."

I didn't know how, but he got me to smile. All I could think was that he was good at flirting – if that was what he was doing.

"Well, there's no need to get too excited; I don't really do art these days."

"Why?"

I looked to my phone, thinking I would see my stopwatch, but I remembered I hadn't set it. Part of me wanted to know how long I'd been there. Not that I was keeping a record.

"OK, answer me this one last thing, then you're free to leave," Kai said.

"I wasn't free to leave before?"

"No. Obviously I was holding you captive, locked in this secret force-field bubble and it will only evaporate if you answer this one last thing."

"Proceed, captor."

"When are we hanging out again?"

"What?"

"Well I only assume we are because of your earlier responses to my questions and because I *know* you're intrigued by me and my *mysteriousness* and you know I'm interested in you. I know we'll be seeing each other again. I can feel it in my gut."

"Really?"

"Yeah. I know you sat there agreeing with everything I just said. Now please answer the question so I can pencil-in the date and plan the perfect second date."

"*Second* date? When was the *first?*"

Kai smirked. He lifted his palms and stretched his arms as if he were offering me our surroundings. "We're in it."

"This is your idea of a first date?"

"Well it *was* short notice. We could've done something else, gone somewhere a little more exciting if you were willing to ride on my motorbike. So when will our perfect second date be?"

I don't know what came over me, but I answered with the first day and time that came to mind, even though I wasn't convinced of my attendance. "Friday. Seven o'clock."

"Two days from now … not much time to prepare, but I like a challenge."

Half of me wanted to go on the date. The other half didn't. I tried to convince myself I was completely uninterested, but I was intrigued. Intrigued to see what he would plan for us. I didn't know what it was about him, but he had me aflame. "Friday."

"See you then, Peyton Swift."

I smiled at him. Partly because my system was struck with a spark of excitement and partly because I liked the way he said my name.

I shifted from the park bench and wandered home.

The clouds clashed together. The sound of thunder rumbled through my ears. Lightning struck, brightening the sky for mere seconds. Rain poured. It was like the weather was repainting another layer of grey – I liked that. I felt content. Almost protected. I made my way home as fast as I could, with my jacket sprawled over my head. I was cold, caught in the storm, but was I wrong to think every cloud has a silver lining?

Chapter TEN

I don't know how it happened, but I found myself sitting across from Dr Wilson. His magical grey eyes smiled at me. This wasn't part of my plan. I had agreed to two sessions. Yet there I was, in his office, for my third. Maybe Mum was better at convincing me to do things than I thought.

"Hi Peyton, how are you today?"

"I'm OK … You?"

"I'm very well thank you."

I bit my lip. Thoughts crashed through my brain. "Can I ask you something?"

"Of course."

"Do you think this is a waste of time? I still don't remember the day of the accident, or the crash itself for that matter … Shouldn't we wait until I remember something?"

"Not necessarily, Peyton. Speaking about your past, your present and future events might help you remember. It might spark memories. It might clear your thoughts and allow you to see."

But I didn't want to see.

"During our last session we spoke about your passion for painting and art. Have you created anything since we last saw one another?"

"No. Art's not really an interest at the moment." When I painted, I used to paint honestly. What I could see. What I wanted to see. I would intertwine my secrets within a piece and wondered if anyone would uncover them or understand the hidden meaning. They never did, and I felt relieved knowing I was still their secret keeper.

"At home, the garage is my art space ... I call it my Art Cave. My mum bought me all the materials I wanted and needed and I would go in there to clear my mind. Escape things. Create things. But I haven't been in there since I've been home."

"And why do you think that is?"

"Um ..." *Because my deepest secret's in there and once I see it I'll have to remember everything else. I'd have to remember. Refeel the pain.* "I haven't had the energy to think about painting ... My creative juices haven't been flowing."

What I said was the truth. But I was never going to speak about my deepest secrets. *I didn't know if I ever could. I didn't know if I ever would.*

The flashes crept. I folded one leg over the other and twisted my calves until my ankles locked – the lower half of my body felt like a decorative pastry. I squeezed my legs together, hoping to cut the circulation. Make my mind focus on something else.

My short-lived attempt was unsuccessful. I untied my legs and readjusted in the seat. My heart raced. The room felt cold. I shook my head. Hoped the flashes would detach. *Darkness. I wanted my darkness.* I thought to the pitch black – my almost-serenity place.

The flashes dissipated. Vanished. As if they had never been mine. The beat of my heart slowed. The room warmed. My brain registered my body as mine. My eyes searched the plain room and recognised where I was – still in therapy. I peered at the clock. Thirty-five minutes remaining. I breathed deeply then faced Dr Wilson – ready for the next question.

Please help keep my mind from those unfinished thoughts.

Dr Wilson cleared his throat, even though I didn't think he needed to.

"During our last session you mentioned you dropped out of school ..." His rich voice remained warm and neutral – like he hadn't witnessed the past few seconds. As if they never happened. Part of me was thankful. Relieved even. "Would you like to discuss that further?"

"Not really ... I dropped out because I didn't want to be there. I couldn't handle it there." Without consent, every muscle in my body tightened. My heart skipped a beat. "I don't want to talk about that."

"OK."

Before he could come up with another question that might spark the flashes, I decided to blurt out words. We still had half an hour left of our session and I didn't want him to dig around any further. "I met this guy."

"Oh, that's nice. What's he like? Tell me about him."

Really? I softly shook my head and played along. I knew I could stretch the subject out for at least twenty minutes. And I would be speaking about someone else. That made me feel a little better.

"I met him the other day … We sat, we chatted. Somehow he made me laugh. Something I haven't done in a while. We bumped into one another again and went on our supposed first date … He's different to other boys I've met. Well, he seems different. He's intriguing and he's honest. But I can feel that I have my guard up around him. Around everyone."

Dr Wilson was good. Somehow – without a single word – he made me shift the boy talk and turn it back to me. Maybe it was because I was in a therapy room and there was something they put in the air to make you confess your deepest thoughts and feelings.

"Why do you think that is?" Dr Wilson asked.

"What?"

"Why do you feel like you have to have your guard up around everyone?"

I pressed on one of my scabs. I wanted to feel a little pain. *Was it worth sharing a little with him?* It couldn't change anything. I took a breath. My words were whispers.

"Sometimes it makes things easier." I didn't want our conversation to follow this path. I licked my lips as I silently listed things I knew about Kai. "But that boy I met, um, he's eighteen and acts like he can get whatever he wants. He's interesting and curious and I can't help but want to know more about him."

"That's great, Peyton. Meeting new people can be a wondrous thing."

Our session ended.

Dr Wilson told me he'd see me next week, and I hated to admit it, but I knew I would be back.

Chapter ELEVEN

I found myself in front of the garage door. The one connected to the inside of the house. The door that took me to my Art Cave. I stood perfectly still. I felt every beat my heart made. I was home alone. The silence lingered.

What was I doing? I knew I wasn't going to go in there, but that was the closest I'd been to the garage since I'd been home. No one else goes in there, so no one else knew and I thanked the heavens above for a family that respected my privacy – most of the time.

My skin began to tingle. Flashes corrupted my mind. Hurriedly making my way to my bedroom, I switched my music on and turned up the volume as loud as it could go. I stood there with my eyes closed as the noise took over every part of me. I didn't fight it. I wanted the sound to drown my thoughts. Drown me. I wanted the music to take me away. Make me forget.

I didn't want to remember. I didn't want to see the light.

It was Friday. Mum was thrilled to find out that I was going on a date with Kai. I tried to play it cool and said we were just hanging out, but she wouldn't have it. I was going on a date. It could only be a date. I started to think that she just liked the word "date". I let her have her moment to bask in the glory that I was getting back out there. I preferred that side of Mum, compared to when she acted as if I was a china doll. Fragile. On the verge of shattering. Sure, I had been injured and the marks across my skin were a daily reminder of the thought of losing me, but there I was in front of her. Alive. *I still think that's what I wanted.* There I was getting ready for the date.

Butterflies swirled within me. A larger part of me regretted agreeing to the date. Was this what I wanted? Was it something I could do? When had I fully convinced myself to commit?

I dressed casual in black jeans and a baggy grey jumper, twisted an extra-large scarf around my neck and arranged a beanie on my head. I platted my hair and let it fall to the side. I tried to cover my nervousness. I didn't want it as an accessory, but no matter how hard I tried, I couldn't shake it away. Mum told me I looked beautiful, but I never saw myself that way.

The doorbell rang.

There he was. Jeans, white t-shirt and his leather jacket. My heart dropped at the thought of the motorbike. I think he saw the concern printed over my face.

"Cool your jets, Peyton," he whispered. "I didn't come here

on my motorbike. I assumed 'not today' either." Kai smiled at me with his wide smile. It was impossible for me not to feel relieved. *Was I really that obvious though?*

"You look nice by the way … Are you ready to go?"

"Yeah … Just let me say goodbye to Mum." I knew she was lingering near the lounge door, listening to every word. Her sudden appearance made that abundantly clear.

"Hi, I'm Kai." He remained on the doorstep and stuck his hand out. "It's nice to see you again."

Mum shook his hand and introduced herself. "I'm Emma. It's nice to see you again, too."

"My intentions with your daughter are as follows: she intrigues me so I must know more. I want to impress her and take her on the best second date she's ever been on to convince her for a third." He looked at me. "Yes, a third. She interests me like no one else ever has. I shall keep her safe, Ms Swift. She will be home at an appropriate hour and I will act like a complete gentleman, like I was born in the fifties, maybe a little more modern – you know, with less sexism and all that, but a gentleman nonetheless."

Was that what he meant by preparing for a second date – impressing my mum?

"Well then, I'll leave you two to it … And no later than eleven would be an appropriate hour."

I'd never had a curfew – I knew Mum was testing him.

"Ten thirty it is then," Kai said.

The nerves stroking through me had partially left when I saw Kai at my door. There was something about him that made me feel almost safe. I wasn't fully ready to acknowledge the excitement I was beginning to feel, but I knew it was there. I still needed my dark sanctuary, unwilling to breathe life into the colours happiness could bring. I took a deep breath and hoped Kai hadn't noticed the internal battle I was waging.

We walked to a rusty tin with wheels, which I assumed was his car. He opened the door for me. I stood frozen on the driveway. The fears I'd been ignoring sprang to the surface. I wanted to get in the car – if only to sit. But I couldn't move.

"Is everything OK?" Kai asked.

I didn't look at him, but felt his stare. My eyes remained locked to his car – a gaze I could not break. My breaths became shallow as the lump grew in my throat.

"The car works perfectly fine I promise. She may look a little rusty but she was, *is*, in tip top shape."

I shook my head and cleared my throat. The words slipped out of my mouth. "I was in a car crash."

I didn't want to tell him. It was never my plan to chuck that in his face. I didn't want to see sympathy sitting in his eyes. I didn't want him to feel bad for me.

For the first time since leaving my house, I looked at him, my sights finally free from gazing at the car. Somehow, I felt like I could breathe a little easier.

"Oh … I'm sorry." Everything changed about him. His body language. His face. His eyes. "We don't have to drive if you don't want … How do you feel about walking?"

A fresh gust of wind pushed between us. I knew a storm

was about to begin. I didn't want to be the reason we caught pneumonia.

"No. I've been in a car since it happened … I … I just haven't been driving with someone other than my mum."

"Well I promise to take it slow. I'll drive at a speed you feel comfortable with. If you want to stop you say the word and we'll stop. I don't care where we are, I'll pull over and we can figure it out … Our date destination isn't far from here anyway. Like I said, we can walk there if you prefer. These boots are made for walking …" Kai lifted his foot, his high-top black boots looked like they might break at any second.

"No … We can drive there."

"Well OK then, whenever you're ready, Miss Swift."

He remained a modern gentleman and held onto the door. I stepped inside and buckled up as he gently shut the door. He walked to the other side and got behind the wheel. "Are you OK?"

"Yeah."

No.

Maybe.

Kai started the car. The engine roared. It was much louder than I anticipated. I jumped at the sound and reached for the dashboard. Kai looked at me. Worry splattered across his face. *I didn't want his sympathy.*

"Are you all right? Do you want me to shut it off?"

I shook my head and rearranged my scarf. "No." I stroked my thighs and breathed deeply. I focused forward to the road ahead. "Just go slow."

He pulled off the kerb. The motion was bumpy and rough. The wheels were flat on the road. We began to move. If I'd closed my eyes I could've pretended I was rollerblading – not that I'd done that since I was a kid – but that's what the drive down the street felt like.

"Is this OK?" Kai asked.

"You can go a little quicker, if you want."

"Dare devil. I like it."

He placed his foot down on the pedal and we moved a little faster. If our windows had been down, there would have been a soft breeze.

The roads were quiet; it made me feel a little safer. During the short drive there wasn't much conversation, other than Kai asking if I was OK and me replying "Yes". The radio kept cutting out. Kai tried to find a signal and change the station. He didn't try for very long. I could tell he wanted to completely focus on driving. My ears latched onto the crackling, then the songs whispered through the speakers. It was a distraction. I turned it into a game to keep myself occupied.

It wasn't until we parked the car that I realised where we were. Through the window, I searched the empty carpark. *Why were we there? There of all places.*

My old high school.

For our second date he took me to a place I promised myself I would never go again.

"What are we doing here?"

"Well I think it would be fun to break in and hang out in there," Kai said.

"Why? That doesn't sound like much fun."

"Have you ever done it before?"

"No."

"Then it's a new experience for both of us!"

"You've never done it before *either*?"

"No, I have. But I've never broken into a school with *you* before."

"And I don't think you will. I don't want to."

"Why?" Kai asked.

"I just don't want to."

"You've gotta give me a reason."

"This is my old high school, Kai! I dropped out a little while ago and promised myself I'd *never* come back here."

"Well, we can make an exception – have you ever seen the school at night?"

"I don't want to!"

"Come on …"

"Is this what you do? Push people to do things they don't want to just so *you* can feel like you're *living*."

"That's not why we're here."

"Why then?"

"I planned our perfect second date. There are things waiting for you in there."

"*Things*? Like *what*?"

"Well it's all supposed to be a surprise."

"Another thing you should know about me. I *don't* like surprises."

"Got it."

"You either tell me what you've planned in there or you take me home."

Kai sighed. He turned the key in the ignition. The engine rumbled. That time I was ready for the sound. We drove back to my house in silence. The radio didn't try to make a noise. Kai didn't even ask me if I was OK. *Maybe he didn't care anymore.*

The sky continued its darkening act. The minutes passed and I grew angrier. Frustrated. Part of me wanted to know what he had planned for me in there. *Was it sexual? Was it supposed to be romantic?* The other part of me just wanted to get out of the car and never see him again.

Kai pulled into my driveway. As I unbuckled, he jumped out of the car and came to the passenger side. I flung open the door before he had a chance to try and woo me with his charm.

"This was the worst best second date I've ever been on!"

"In my mind it didn't play out like this …"

"Well not *everything* in life can be planned out … Goodbye Kai Pearson." I stormed off before he could say anything else. He could have called out as I walked to the front door, but he didn't.

Slamming the door released some of the anger I carried. My heart sank. *Was I disappointed?* I made my way to the lounge and peeked out the window. I stared at him. He was looking to the stars, his shoulders raised as he breathed deeply. He closed the passenger door then made his way to the driver's seat. The car engine grumbled and made me jump. The headlights shone as he reversed away.

I closed the curtains. My heart grew heavy. *I was disappointed.*

"P, what are you doing back so early?"

"I wasn't in the mood for a date. I'm just going to go to bed."

"Is everything all right? Are you all right?"

"Yeah. It's fine. I'm fine."

"Did something happen?"

"Mum, I just want to go to bed. Night."

I felt weighted as I closed my bedroom door. I couldn't stop my hands trembling. They'd been like that since the accident, but it was starting to go away. It wasn't until I noticed that the rest of me was shaking that I realised I wasn't trembling because of a side effect. My bones were clattering because I was remembering.

My breaths were scattered. Through teary eyes I searched for a distraction. But my mind wasn't letting me latch onto anything other than the flashes, which grew stronger with every short breath. I bit my lip and shook my head. I remembered the sound of the door locking. It was abnormally loud. I was frozen. Trapped. I remembered running with nowhere to run.

A tear rolled down my chin. I'd known since I'd been home from hospital that my bedroom was no longer my sanctuary. I hated the fact that this place where I could once find countless distractions no longer offered me one in my greatest time of need. I shut my eyes and clasped my hands around my head, pretending that that would cut my thoughts short. But I remembered the blinds being shut. I remembered screaming to no one.

I opened my eyes and searched my bedroom. For a moment it felt like I was back there – in that room. I twisted my door handle and cracked open the door. I could get out. I could run. I could run to Mum – if I wanted. I could tell her. I shut my door and lent against it. Every part of me shook.

I squeezed my arm. Pressed onto the largest cut I had. I squeezed harder and harder until my entire thoughts had to focus on the pain. I took slow deeps breaths in my final attempt to take back control of my thought pattern.

The physical pain was all I could feel. I throbbed. My heart. My brain. My arm.

I placed myself on the edge of my bed. My hand still resting on my injury – ready to squeeze if a hint of my past flashed.

I wished I had known Kai was going to take me to my old school. I could've stopped him. I could've stopped this. I knew going on the date was a bad idea. My darkness would've been easier to crawl into if I hadn't of spent so much time with his light.

Chapter TWELVE

I woke from a nightmare. This time I didn't forget it. How could I? I had already remembered so much last night. I sprang upright. Panted. I clutched my blankets and raised them to my chin. My jaw trembled. Tears rolled down my cheek. I knew it wasn't a nightmare. It was my reality. My past. My secret.

Sobbing into my sheets, I didn't want my crying to wake Mum. I didn't want her to see me like that. I couldn't let her see me like that. I knew she thought I was starting to feel better. I didn't want to taint her hope for me.

I dried my eyes and cheeks. They felt raw from previous rough wiping. It was 3.02 am. The poisonous thoughts weighed me down. I rested my head on the pillow. Covered my whole body with blankets. Warmth radiated. I breathed deeply to calm myself – keep the recollection at bay. The dark night sheltered me. I just wished it could have halted that nightmare or made it vanish. I closed my eyes, but I knew I wouldn't go back to sleep.

Every session with Dr Wilson he followed my lead of where to sit. I often felt the need to sit somewhere different. This time we sat opposite each other. No desk between us. It made me feel a little more comfortable. But my heart was still unsure. My inner whisperings kept me cautious.

I leant back in the cushioned chair – it's comfort almost reassuring. I stroked my thighs as I peered at Dr Wilson. He was leaning back, his ankle resting on his knee, his fingers linked and resting on his thigh. He was a man in his forties with a calming energy. Casual and welcoming. I believed I could tell him anything, even though I knew I wouldn't tell him everything.

We did our usual welcome: How are you? Fine. How are you?

My mind raced with thoughts of my early-morning recollection. I closed my eyes and sighed, then just blurted out: "Last night I remembered something … something that happened to me … and no matter how hard I try, it won't leave me alone. And even though I know it's real, I know it happened, I don't want to believe it."

Dr Wilson remained still. He didn't speak. He just listened.

I quickly flicked a tear from my eye, hoping he didn't see it. A stitch of nerves locked in my stomach. Their sharpness brought pain. I clutched at my arm and stretched my skin. I was scared to tell him what I remembered. I was scared to tell him the truth. I didn't want the judgement. I didn't want the sympathy. But I wanted it out of my mind. I wanted it off my chest. *Maybe I did have to tell him everything.*

I inhaled a scattered breath. I took a chance. "I haven't told anyone this. Actually I'm still deciding whether I should tell you or not. Things could be easier if I don't, but maybe they could also be easier if I do. My past has been eating away at me for so long … and I thought I could shake it away. I thought I could make it go away. You know? Forget about it. But every time I try, it creeps its way back to me. And after my crash, I thought maybe I had forgotten … I went on a date with that boy, that I told you about, and he took me somewhere, a place I promised myself I'd never go again. He didn't know that, so things didn't go so well. I made him take me home and then my past, it came flooding back … parts of it anyway."

I glanced at Dr Wilson. I knew he knew there was something more going on with me – I could tell by the way his skin curved, his pupils opened. I guess after that little rant he was under the impression there's more to me than my accident.

I didn't know if I could function in the outside, if I left this session without telling him. I averted my eyes from his. Unprepared to watch their sparkle dim. I moved my hands and rested them on my knees. They were shaking. I didn't attempt to stop them.

"I never wanted anyone to know what happened … I thought that I could figure this out on my own. I thought I could fight this on my own. But I don't think I will ever be able to run away from it."

I bit my lip, hard. When the pain hit, I realised we'd been sitting in silence. I was glad Dr Wilson hadn't said anything. If he had, I think I would've lost the will to share as soon as his soothing voice hit my eardrums. I let the sound of the rain meeting the windows drown to the background. My chest hurt as I drew breath.

"I was raped."

My body grew numb. I felt a wave of nothingness engulf me. I twiddled my fingers, but I didn't feel the movement. I couldn't feel myself breathe. I pushed down on one of my scabs. I felt nothing. I panicked. "Dr Wilson, *no one* can know. You can't tell *anyone*."

Dr Wilson placed his foot on the floor.

I retreated. The chair nudged backwards.

Guilt smudged over his face. "I'm sorry, Peyton …"

I held my breath. My eyes stared at him. I knew I had just overreacted. I readjusted the chair in silence. "Please promise me you won't tell anyone … I …"

"Peyton, our sessions are strictly confidential."

"*Promise* me you won't tell."

Dr Wilson put his hand to his chest. "I promise."

I needed to hear him say those exact words. It made me feel as though it was still my secret to keep, to lock up and throw away the key. But now maybe having another pair of hands to hold the burden would help me.

"Peyton, are you comfortable to discuss what happened to you in any further detail?"

In my mind I repeated his question. "I don't remember everything, just that it happened."

He began to take a breath, ease his way into another question, but before he could speak, I cut him off. "Can we talk about something else, now?"

"This is something we should talk about in more depth, but right now, if talking about something else will make you feel more comfortable, of course." He leant back in his chair. *I think he was disappointed.*

I should have had a subject ready to change to.

"Um, I think I hate that boy I met. The one I told you about last week … I think we broke up, even though we weren't really together … Is it weird or wrong if I do breakup-type things? You know, burn the clothing he saw me in or write a list of reasons why I hate him."

"Grieving the end of a relationship is a natural occurrence and we all grieve differently."

"But I wouldn't call what we had a relationship … We met, then went our separate ways in a matter of ninety-six hours, give or take."

"But you experienced the beginning and the end of something."

"I don't really know what that's supposed to mean. He did this surprise thing for me. I don't like surprises. I like to know things. I like to be prepared. But I don't feel like I'm prepared for anything anymore. Not since what happened to me and then the accident."

There they were. His grey eyes. They looked into me deeper, silently begging me to continue. Begging me to open up my thoughts and feelings. I already had. I couldn't go any further. Not in that session. I had told him what I remembered. What was part of my past – my truth. I had confessed what I didn't want to believe.

Dr Wilson looked at me softly. I wasn't going to give in.

"That surprise he did for me, I want to know what it was."

He nodded. *I knew he was disappointed – again.*

"I know this all sounds mysterious, me not telling you names or locations. But I don't know what was supposed to happen or how I'm supposed to feel."

"Sometimes, Peyton, not knowing can be a good thing. But discovering new feelings and allowing yourself to embrace such emotion could be beneficial."

Sometimes I hated the therapy sessions. Dr Wilson always answered my questions or provided advice so cryptically. I felt even more confused with what I should or shouldn't do with myself.

My eyes found the clock. Time was up. The session had finished. I glanced at him.

"I think we're done for today, Peyton. Unless there is anything else you would like to discuss."

I bit my lip and shook my head.

"OK then. I shall see you next week."

"Bye." I left his office. The door clicked closed. A weight lifted off my shoulders. I took a breath. *That wasn't so bad.*

Chapter THIRTEEN

A cold raindrop hit my cheek and shook me from my daze. I looked to my phone for the time. I was going to set my stopwatch, but it was too late. I was already out in the open. I didn't have the strength to focus on anything other than surviving outside – around other people. My desire for an answer about what Kai had planned for us had dwindled. I didn't want to have anything to do with him. I didn't want to be around him. I didn't want to be around myself.

Earlier that morning, Mum and I were on the phone with a lawyer. She said that she was working on getting me a Good Behaviour Bond. I glanced at Mum and shared her concerns. Guilt weighed on me because of all the costs. I didn't mean for this to happen.

The rain continued to fall but I was glad I hadn't brought an umbrella. The pain medication I had taken this morning was working too well. In my own twisted way, I wanted to feel the pain from my wounds. Dr Enderson advised me that walking would be good for my limbs. He said staying mobile would help me. But today, taking the medication and losing that feeling of pain, only made my mind return to what I remembered. Having no physical pain meant there was no distraction.

I decided to avoid the coffee shop. I didn't want to see Kai. It was too risky. So I walked to the other side of town. I never usually went that far. There was not much to see. For the past year and a half that area had been under renovation. Recently there was a lot of hype in the community because it was announced the shops would be opening soon. Mum couldn't wait to do more shopping. I, on the other hand, wasn't fazed.

The damp streets were empty. As the days passed the temperature had dropped and I was happy it was winter. The coldness was something I liked.

I made my way past the newly wooden-framed windows. The stores stretched down the street, side by side. Some were still empty, others were being filled and storekeepers were arranging their front windows. I continued slowly down the street, inhaling the thick smell of rain and paint mixed with wood shavings. The air stung my lungs. But the feeling didn't last long enough for me to latch onto the distraction.

Stepping over the cracks, trying to not fall through, wasn't working for me either. I looked up and couldn't believe it. What was he doing there?

As our eyes met, I froze like an ice statue. He took one step in my direction and I swivelled around trying to skip away. I tripped over myself. My hands smashed onto the cold asphalt and began to throb. I grinned at the feeling. The distraction.

I heard feet jog towards me.

"Peyton, are you all right?"

"I'm fine." I was never usually that clumsy.

Kai reached out his hand. "Here, let me help you up."

"I've got it." I pushed myself up then patted down my soggy clothes.

"So what brings you to this side of town?"

Trying to avoid you.

"You're visiting the enemy aren't you? And by enemy I mean the new coffee shop that's opening a few doors down from here. Because the one I work at, it has class, tradition … better coffee. I mean this one is … I don't think it suits your style … and I mean … it *stinks* of fresh paint."

"I see you've sussed out the enemy then."

"I may have stepped inside for a brief moment. I went in undercover, like a secret investigator, to check out the competition."

A car rushed past us. I flinched. I closed my eyes and focused on my throbbing hands. The feeling was dwindling. The distraction was slowly ending. I couldn't look Kai in the eyes; his brightness was overwhelming.

"Peyton, are you OK?"

"Yeah, I just … I've got to get home."

"Well, let me give you a lift. There's a storm brewing and I'd hate to think that you were out in it … that I left you in it."

"Thanks Kai, but I really need the walk."

"Well let me walk with you."

I separated my lips to respond – kindly declining his offer – then realised during these past few seconds my mind hadn't wandered to my past. The throbbing had vanished but I had a new distraction.

"What about if we walk to my car? It's just up the road … the same direction you'd be walking." He smiled.

"OK."

Kai and I strolled side by side.

"So what were you doing this side of town? You were checking out the new coffee shop, weren't you? Be honest … I can take it."

"I actually forgot there was a new coffee shop opening. I just wanted some new scenery, that's all."

We continued to stroll. A mist of rain descended.

"Kai?"

"Yeah?"

"What was in the school? What did you plan for us?"

Kai kept his sights ahead. The seconds dragged before he answered. "We didn't go in, so it doesn't matter."

"I want to know. *Please*."

"Why?"

"Because since my accident I've felt like a broken puzzle. Part of me doesn't want to find the missing pieces, because they're not missing at all. I know *exactly* where they are … But *please*, don't take away *another* piece." I fought the tears that pricked my eyes and composed my breathing. I felt him turn to me. I could tell he was deciding whether to give me the real answer or not. I didn't look at him. I was beginning to slowly crumble. Retreat. I didn't want him to see me cry.

Kai took a breath. To my relief he spoke. All the energy I was focusing on keeping myself together was redirected to his words.

"I broke into an art room half an hour or so earlier. I took a picnic basket, set the food on the table, along with candles – unlit I might add. I'm not *that* stupid. I was going to ask you to close your eyes then I could light them so you saw everything in candlelight. You would have all the art essentials you needed to create something and show me your mad art skills. And I say that without seeing a piece of your work. We would have shared stories, secrets maybe. And I would've asked you for a third date."

His words cut me, although I knew that was not their intention. Yet they'd officially been added to the collection of injuries I already wore. In that moment, I felt even worse. The conversation felt like it would accomplish nothing, other than prove I was a selfish person. I felt like I had just butchered this guy's hard work. He did all of that to impress me, and without even seeing it, without even experiencing it, I was impressed. Nobody had ever gone to as much trouble to do anything like that for me before.

"I'm sorry … I ruined it all."

"No you didn't."

I turned to him. "You don't have to act all nice about it. Yes, I did. I ruined your plans. All your hard work."

"Yeah, OK." Kai snickered. "You kind of did. But you

must have had a good reason. I could see you hate that place. I'm sorry I made you feel like I was pushing you … If I had known it was your old school and you never wanted to go there again we wouldn't have ended up there. I guess I didn't want to take no for an answer 'cause I wanted you to see it."

We stopped at his car.

I guess I've spoilt things. I've spoilt this. Whatever this was. "Well, at least now you don't have to ask me for that third date."

"What? The third date is still happening," he spluttered.

"But it's been a week and we haven't even …"

"You've just made me have to think a little harder. Plan something you most certainly cannot say no to. Which reminds me, we've been on one pre-date, two actual dates, even though the second one wasn't fully followed through, and we haven't even exchanged numbers. Hand me your phone."

A bubble of happiness jolted through me. A feeling I didn't anticipate. A feeling I was unprepared for. A colour I wasn't expecting. The distraction was working, so I continued to play along. We exchanged numbers. My stomach fluttered.

"I'm going to continue my stroll." I awkwardly pointed in no given direction.

"Oh, all right then. You sure you don't want to me drop you home?"

"I'm sure. But thanks."

I continued walking. My phone rang. I looked at the name

displayed. I couldn't stop the corners of my mouth from lifting. "Hello."

"Hi. It's Kai."

"Hi."

"I just wanted to make sure I have the right number and that you still want to go on our third date."

"You mean you wanted to check if I gave you my real number?"

"I just didn't want it to be wrong, that's all."

"OK, well, is this proof enough?" I stopped walking away and turned to face him and half-heartedly raised my hand to wave.

I heard his small breathy laugh. "Yeah."

"Well I better get home now…"

"OK. Bye."

I walked home with a smile stencilled on my face. I played our conversation over and over again. This distraction was sweeter than the ones I caused myself. I scrolled through the list of contacts and found his name, then clicked on it.

Me: Yes, by the way.

Kai: To what?

Me: Going on our third date.

Kai: Just tell me when. And maybe u choose where this time. I'll bring the rest.

Chapter FOURTEEN

It was late morning. I was bored. I had done my usual morning act, which felt like a daily ritual. Eat breakfast – which consisted of sprinkling some flakes or oats in a bowl and drowning them with milk. I sat at the kitchen table, soaked in silence, and carelessly swirled the spoon as if I were hypnotised. I usually ate a few spoonfuls until my body insisted I was full or not hungry. I'd throw the sloppy cereal away, then empty the dishwasher. After that I'd make my way down the hall. Mum had arranged frames on the wall. They were filled with some of our favourite family moments. Photographs of when Liam and I were babies. A close-up family selfie taken just over a year ago, our three smiles wide and bright. I stared at the picture. My heart swelled, yet I wondered if I'd ever feel as much happiness as had been captured in that photo.

My grey state took over. My body grew numb. I sombrely walked to the bathroom, brushed my teeth and washed my face. I barely looked at myself in the mirror. I could count on one hand how many times I had stared at myself – really looked at myself – since returning home from hospital. That day was no different. The mirror offered me no interest. I didn't know who I really was anymore, and right now I wasn't curious to find out. I didn't really want to see my face. Since being home I would close my eyes as I dressed myself, so there was no chance to catch a glimpse of my healing wounds. *Would they ever be beautiful?* At that time I didn't really care. They were there for one purpose and one purpose only. The time I would look at them was when I'd pick at them in the shower. Force a speck of pain. Then let the water wash it away. I wasn't sure if I wanted to see the marks that day. I wasn't sure if I was ready.

My ears latched on to the sound of a passing car. The humming of its engine and the rush of tyres lasted for just seconds. The brief noise was a welcome change. I opened my eyes and took a deep breath as I searched my bedroom. The turquoise feature wall was fading and chipping. I kept my blinds closed to keep the darkness. For a change I had made my bed and arranged my cushions. The smell of vanilla, from a large candle Mum bought me last Christmas, stuck in my nostrils. I liked the aroma – simple and sweet.

I flopped on my bed. Home alone again. I liked being by myself. I didn't have to put on a show or convince someone I was fine. I knew Mum knew there was something going on, that I wasn't the same girl from several months ago – the girl who was slightly outgoing and dreamt of exploring the world. I think she believed the therapy sessions were helping.

That was also why I still went to them – because it was helping her.

I stared at the ceiling, silently questioning what I was doing with myself. What I should be doing with myself. A small speck of me missed school. Missed the regularity of it all.

What was I thinking? I hated that place. I never wanted to go back.

Without warning, memories flashed. They arrived so quickly that I couldn't shake them away. All I could see were eyes filled with hatred. The trickle of blood. Blurred movements. I wanted to scream. A sharp pain stung my chest. I couldn't breathe. I rushed to leave my bedroom. Searched for an escape. I stumbled down the hall, leaving the vanilla scent behind, and hurriedly made my way outside. The fresh air met me. I wheezed in the cold. The imagery vanished. I fell to the ground. Defeated. I inhaled slowly until my wheezing became controlled breaths. Rain grazed my skin. It felt heavier as the seconds passed. But it could have been the collection of tears that rested on my cheeks. I crouched on the grass and wished I could be cleansed of the secret I was keeping. Cleansed of this part of me I didn't want. The part of me I tried to forget.

I wasn't entirely ready for our date, although this time I was determined not to ruin it. I had begun to overanalyse the appropriateness of this moment. Because of what had happened to me, I wasn't totally ready for this moment. Was it something I could handle? It kind of helped that I knew where we were going. Still, nerves sauntered through me. There was still time to cancel. But I knew if I did, I wouldn't have a distraction.

The doorbell rang. Mum answered it as I sat on the sofa and laced up my shoes.

"Hello Ms Swift."

"Hi Kai. And please, just call me Emma."

I made my way to the front door. The three of us stood together.

"My intensions with your daughter remain the same. Although this time round, I'm determined to give her the best third date."

Mum smiled her beautiful smile. I could tell she liked him, which kind of made this easier. "Off with you two."

Kai wore his black leather jacket and black jeans with a dark-green V-neck t-shirt and a black fedora, which suited him perfectly. His slightly curly hair was slicked back, revealing his fresh forehead. The ends of his hair fell just above his shoulders. He looked hotter than I remembered. I was unprepared for the colours he exuded. Unprepared for the light he radiated.

"Ready for round three?" His cheeky smile stretched across his face.

We arrived at my chosen destination. His tin can of a car got us there safely. We strolled into the ice-cream restaurant. It looked like it had been built in the 1950s – bright red fake-leather booths near the walls, small round two-seater tables arranged on the floor. We walked inside. Music played. Mum, Liam and I had been there every year on the first day of summer until we had grown out of the tradition. It was sad, really. I felt like I was missing out. But I knew I would always have those happy memories.

There was a crowd of people, and I was thankful; I needed them to be there.

Kai and I strolled to the counter. There were rows of tubs of different flavoured ice-cream and containers filled with too many types of toppings and sauces to count.

"So why here?" Kai asked.

I looked up at him. He was the perfect height. I could stand on my tiptoes and steal a kiss from him, if I wanted. I shook the idea from my thoughts. Tried to make it look like I was adjusting my hair through a flick.

"Have you never been here?"

"No." Kai shook his head and slightly scrunched his nose and lips.

I liked it when he did that.

"Well, I haven't been here in a long time and I have so many fond memories of this place, I thought it would be nice to come back here. Years ago, coming here was a treat. One my brother and I couldn't wait for. Mum would let us order anything we wanted. One time, the three of us shared the Gigantor. It was supposed to be a challenge for just one person, and if they finished it all, they would get free ice-cream from the shop for a whole year. We took on the challenge and devoured it all. The owners were the nicest couple and gave my brother and me a little prize for eating it all, even though it was kind of cheating." I smiled to myself. Right then, in that moment, I missed being a kid. I missed having no responsibilities. No worries. I also missed Liam and decided to text him when I got home.

Kai and I ordered our ice-creams then made our way to an empty booth. The spongy seats were just like I remembered, but the table felt lower.

We ate our frozen desserts.

"Tell me something," Kai said.

"What do you want to know?"

"Everything. Anything." He licked his spoon clean.

I bit my bottom lip. *Was that because I wanted to kiss him? Or was it just an act of nerves?* All I knew was that he wanted to know about me, and I wasn't sure if I wanted him to. What would happen if he didn't like what he saw? I was glad of the dark, baggy clothes I wore. They were layers that shielded me.

"Um …" I gazed around the room and thought of the first thing that came to mind – other than wanting know what it would be like to kiss him. "I'm a winter type of girl."

"And what does that mean?"

"I prefer it when it's winter."

He stayed quiet, making me feel the need to elaborate.

"I love to snuggle with a blanket and listen to the rain as it falls. I like the sound the branches make when the wind rushes through them. If you listen carefully, it's like they're whispering to one another,"

I couldn't believe I just said that. That must've sounded so lame.

"What about you?" I shoved a huge spoonful of ice-cream into my mouth so words could no longer exit.

"What? Do *I* like winter?"

I nodded as I tried to mumble through my mouthful.

"I like all seasons. Some more than others. Summer's my favourite though."

We finished our ice-creams but remained at the booth and continued to talk. I felt like I was the only girl in the world. Like at that very moment we were the only two people in the world. When I spoke he was always intrigued. He always wanted to know more. Every side of what I thought. I could tell he just wanted to understand. He looked at me and only me. Other customers walked into the restaurant – families with their boisterous children, other high schoolers – girls much prettier than me. From the corner of my eye I saw them check him out, silently wondering what was someone like him doing with someone like me. But his attention never strayed.

"Are you up for a walk?" Kai asked.

I peered out the window and saw the streets weren't empty. I eased up a little. I knew the night's air would be thin and cold, but I agreed to the walk anyway. I slightly feared if I didn't, then he would just drive me home and our third date would be over – and I didn't want the date to be over. I was enjoying myself.

We strolled side by side. The air wasn't as cold as I was prepared for, but I knew as the minutes passed the temperature would decrease and the air would become crisp. We would look like two ice-breathing dragons.

"Tell me about your family. What's your brother like? Your mum? Your dad?" Kai said.

"Well, we don't speak about my dad … He ditched us when we were really young and we haven't seen him since."

"I'm gonna go ahead and say he's a jerk. I won't say the real words I'm thinking, they're not for young ears. But he'll never be brought up again."

"You're only a year older than me."

"Still, he's a topic we don't need to discuss. He clearly doesn't know what he's missing out on. On to the next thing. What about your brother? What's he like?"

"His name's Liam. He's been at college a little while now, studying business. He's a couple of years older than me and has these ocean-blue eyes. If you stare long enough it's like you can see waves. We did too many staring-eye contests when we were kids. Actually, when I was younger I used to want his eyes; mine are a darker blue like my mum's, but I don't think I'd be able to pull his off. He's about as tall as you, maybe a little taller and his right arm is covered with tattoos, one of which *I* designed. I drew this picture ages ago and showed him one night. He thought it was awesome. He told me he wanted it, said he was going to frame it and put it in his room. I told him that it wasn't finished yet. Without me knowing, he went into my Art Cave and stole it. He asked the tattooist to permanently print it on his skin. When he showed me I couldn't believe it. He loved my drawing so much he had it inked on him. I knew he was making a point, proving that my art was good enough to show the world. And now it's a piece in his story sleeve. I love him to bits, even when we get into stupid arguments, but they vanish minutes later and then we're best friends again."

"He sounds like a pretty cool guy…"

"He is."

"Do you think you don't do art anymore because Liam's not around to show it to?"

"No not really. I know I can draw or paint anything and show him. Take a picture, email him, FaceTime him. But I've not been in a creative mood lately."

"Well, I'm no Liam, but I will happily stand in as substitute viewer of your artworks."

"Thanks." I chuckled. "I'll keep that in mind…"

"Please do. I'm at your beck and call."

I smiled.

"So what about your mum? What's she like? I know I've already met her, and she's great. But tell me more."

"Well, my mum is amazing. We get along like we're two peas in a pod. We laugh at each other's lame jokes, watch movies and TV shows together. I understand what she's saying when she mumbles with her mouth filled with food and she understands me when I do the same. We share secrets. Dreams. Hopes. She's protective and is not afraid to transform into a mama bear. She always wants the best for Liam and me and always puts us first. She is the greatest woman I know. Strong. Independent. Beautiful. Confident.

Everything I hope to be one day. I'm lucky to have her and I know that."

I glanced at Kai. He smiled but I saw a speck of hurt in his eyes. Like my words had somehow weakened him. *Was I reading him wrong?* "What about you? Do you have any siblings? What are your parents like?"

Kai shook everything away. "Nah. We're still on you."

For a moment I didn't say anything. The sound of our footsteps took over the conversation. I debated what to say. "But you haven't told me anything about your family. Don't you want to?"

"Maybe another time."

I had never seen him like that before. He was cold and not just because the temperature was decreasing. *I didn't understand.*

"Hey, it's getting pretty cold now. Do you wanna head back to the car? I'll take you home. We should get there around quarter past ten. I think your mum will be impressed." As he spoke his words became fog.

"Um, OK." My words became fog too.

I looked at him, silently questioning why he felt he couldn't tell me something about himself. That whole time he wanted to know everything and anything about me, but I couldn't know about him. He rubbed his hands in front of his chest then blew into them as we quickly made our way to his car. I hoped we walked fast because he wanted to be free of the cold.

We arrived at my house at 10.22 pm. I knew it was that

time exactly because I looked at my phone, wanting to see my stopwatch. But I hadn't set it. Kai walked me to the front door. We stopped and faced one another. Our breath visible. If he was going to lean in for a kiss, I wasn't going to allow it. I wasn't ready. I was never going to allow it, but especially not with the way things had changed. The mood wouldn't have been right.

He took both my hands in his and raised them to his cold lips. My elbows were stiff with resistance but unlocked when he softly placed a kiss on my knuckles and replaced my arms to my sides.

"How was our third date?" Kai smiled, but it wasn't the bright one he usually used. "The best third date you've ever been on?"

"Yeah." I had to say that. That was the only third date I'd been on.

"Goodnight, Peyton Swift. Sweet dreams."

As he walked towards his car, I made my way inside. Mum had the heater on. My limbs began to defrost. I leant against the door and heard his engine roar then hum as he reversed. I didn't like the fact that there was something he wasn't telling me.

Chapter FIFTEEN

I woke from an average night's rest. That morning I didn't wake in a sweat, tangled with my sheets. I dozed in and out of sleep. Wrestled with restlessness. Throughout the night I had peered at my alarm clock, Kai at the front of my mind. *What was he not telling me?*

I got out of bed and grabbed some breakfast. It wasn't much, but at least there was something in my stomach to keep me going through the day – until I had to convince myself to eat something again. I no longer had to take the tablets I was prescribed – I had taken them all. But if anything changed or if I needed something, all I had to do was call Dr Enderson. I had considered asking for another prescription of painkillers, but they didn't stop the memories. They didn't stop the pain in my mind from hurting.

I made myself comfortable on the sofa and turned on the TV, stumbling upon a black-and-white movie. I didn't care what it was about. There were no colours to shade myself from and it made me feel safe. As time passed I became engrossed. The movie mirrored my life. There was a special secret painting that gradually revealed the main character's inner ugliness. I needed to know how it ended so I might prepare myself if it ended the same for me.

My phone beeped.

I smiled when I saw it was a text from Liam.

Liam: Hey P! How u feeling today? xx

Me: Hi Liam. I'm OK. How r u?

Liam: I'm good. What have u been up to?

Me: Therapy. Which Mum is happy about and I'm sure u r too … I met this guy the other day and we went on a date.

Liam: Glad to hear you're doing well. U know u can talk to me whenever u need to. I'm just a text, phone call, video chat away xx

Liam: & who's this guy you've met?!? What's his name?

Me: His name's Kai. He works at the coffee shop we love!

Liam: Do u need me & the guys to suss him out?

Me: I think I'm doing fine by myself. But I will inform u if I need back up.

Liam: OK P. Be good! I've gotta get back to class. Speak soon! xx

Me: Stay outta trouble kid!

I placed my phone on the coffee table and continued to watch the film. The plot was thickening. The main character's conscience was getting the better of him and only a full confession would absolve him from his past. I feared for how long it would be until I could be cleared of my own past. Cleansed from my secret. Was my time for absolution nearing?

My phone beeped.

The sound shook my thoughts that intertwined my reality, that movie and my secret. I took a deep breath. I was becoming good at shifting my thoughts but worried that I would no longer be able to achieve it so easily in front of the ones I cared for. I wondered when I couldn't hide anymore.

I grabbed my phone. It was a text from Kai. There wasn't a single ounce of me that knew what he would write. I couldn't read him like he could me. But I found myself partially smiling, even though my stomach twisted.

Kai: Guitar or ukulele?

Me: What?

He replied immediately.

Kai: Which do u prefer the sound of?

Me: Guitar.

Kai: Excellent choice Miss Swift. Shall we say today 1 pm at our picnic table?

Me: Our picnic table? And which one is that exactly?

I looked at the time – 12.26 pm. He enjoyed spontaneity.

It took him a couple of minutes to respond. I waited impatiently for his colourful reply.

My phone beeped. I opened the new text.

Kai: The one we sat at for our very first date.

I laughed a little. That smile lingered on my face for longer than I predicted. Longer than I expected. I thought back to our first date and it made a feeling spark inside me. *Was I happy?* I decided to halt the over-analyser inside of me. If I didn't, I wouldn't be moving forward. I wouldn't be creating moments. Building forces to help stop me thinking about my past.

Me: See u at 1.
Kai: Bring a blanket!

I wore my black hooded coat, wrapped a thick scarf around my neck and hugged a blanket as I made my way to the picnic table. Our picnic table. The wooden rectangle joined to the two benches at either side. It looked darker than I remembered, perhaps because of the heavy downpour during the night. I folded the blanket long ways and then over again so it was big enough for us to sit on it. I put it on the table then raised myself up and placed my feet on the seat.

Cars passed. The splashing of tyres on wet roads flickered in my ears. A slight breeze shuffled. It wasn't strong enough to send shivers up and down my spine, but still I rubbed my hands over my legs to create some warmth. I turned to the coffee shop and saw Kai wandering towards me. In his right hand he held two takeaway cups in a cardboard tray and in his left hand he held the neck of an acoustic guitar.

He stood at the opposite end of the picnic table. "Good afternoon, Peyton Swift. Did you dream of anything sweet last night?"

No. When my slumber was disturbed I thought of you. When I went back to sleep I don't remember dreaming, only to wake up again and think of you. "Not that I can remember … Did you?"

"Not that I can remember. Dreams are a curious thing. I brought us some hot chocolates. You *do* like hot chocolate, right?"

"Of course I do. What a silly question."

Kai chuckled. "Well good. I brought one with marshmallows, and one without. Which do you prefer?"

"Marshmallows, please." I grabbed the takeaway cup. It was warm in my hands. A new feeling of heat toured my skin. I took a sip. The sweet taste of marshmallows hit my tastebuds. I smiled. It made me think of the many times during winter when Mum made Liam and me hot chocolates layered with mini marshmallows. The three of us snuggled on the sofa, wrapped with blankets as a fake fire sparked on Liam's laptop, and we watched a movie on the television.

I took another sip. The hot liquid warmed my insides. "So, what's with the guitar?"

"Well, you told me you like drawing and painting, but haven't been creative lately. So I thought I would show you something I like doing to help your creative juices flow *and* to encourage you to share some of your artwork with *me*. If I can share my gift of song, then you can *definitely* share a canvas with me."

The notion of sharing my art with another made me feel uneasy. "We'll see."

Kai smiled, then took a sip of his hot chocolate.

"Well, before you play, tell me something. Do you write your own material? And if so, where do you get your inspiration?"

"I dabble in writing lyrics. I'm no game changer to the art. But it helps me see things clearer … And I find inspiration all around. My past, my present, my hopes for my future. My songs are like my little secrets, or lines from the diary I don't actually keep."

Kai's words struck a chord with me. His songs were where he kept his secrets, just as my art was where I kept mine. "OK then. Let me hear a Kai Pearson original."

"I must warn you that when I sing, I sound like a dog that's had its vocal chords surgically removed."

"I thought you said you have the gift of song?"

"Well, that was to entice you to hear me play. Plus, the fact that I sing so terribly and am still willing to share with you this thing I love, should prove to you I am a suitable candidate for humbly viewing your art."

I smiled at him.

"Ready?"

I nodded.

"This song's called 'Follow You'."

I braced myself for the sound I imagined from his description, but what my ears heard wasn't actually that bad. His singing voice was raw, tender and filled with authentic emotion. He was actually really good. I listened to his every word.

I'm gonna follow you, I'm gonna follow you home
Cause I wanna know you, I wanna know you all
I'm gonna follow you, I'm gonna follow you home
Look at the heart of you, I wanna know you all

All of your secrets and all of the times you've cried
Your feeling of misfit and when you're questioning why

I wish I could follow you, I wish I could follow you all
Make my own wings too, I don't wanna let you go
I'll keep my own thoughts of you, yeah I'll keep them all
You know that I love you, I wish I could follow you
I wish I could follow you home

I kept my eyes on him. I wanted to clap. To applaud his heart-filled performance. But it felt so inconsiderate. I felt like he had shown a part of his soul. Something I hoped he hadn't done with anyone else. He had just shared a secret. A part of his past in the shape of a rhyme that was up to me to decode. Then maybe he would feel like he could speak to me about himself. Not just the charming things or his unique perspective on life. But also about things that made him sad. His dark side.

"Wow. That was deep."

We both sipped our hot chocolates.

"It's not entirely finished yet … I know it needs more work. But that's what I've done so far and …"

"You're really good. I like the sound of your voice. If that's what a dog with surgically removed vocal chords sounds like, then I think I have my closing argument to convince my mum we should get a dog."

Kai laughed.

"Thanks for sharing that …"

His phone rang.

"Ah sorry. That's my alarm. I've gotta get back to work." Kai jumped from the table. Before I even had a chance to object, he quickly placed a kiss on my cheek. Not that I was going to object, right then. Not in that moment. He shouted from the coffee-shop door. "I'll text you later!"

The feeling of his lips lingered on my skin. I placed my warmed fingers to my face, holding the kiss there. I didn't want it to be stolen by the cold.

Chapter SIXTEEN

Mum and I were on the sofa. A heavy downpour of rain attacked the windows. The heater was on but I pulled a soft blanket to my chin. We flicked through several channels before she went to work. I didn't pay attention to what was playing. I just stared at the screen, pretending to soak in the scenes.

"How's your head today?" Mum said.

I already knew what direction this conversation was going. I wanted so much to divert it. But I knew she would ask either way.

"It's all right."

"What about your memories? Do you remember anything new?"

I licked my lips. "No."

She set the remote down. I felt her eyes on me. "I don't get why you just couldn't wait for me."

"I don't know; maybe we needed bread or something. I wanted to help out. I wanted to try and do something by myself." I finally looked at her. "I didn't *mean* for it to happen. I'm sorry."

"P, all I care about is that you're safe and alive. I don't care about the car or the cost of a lawyer or whatever else we have to do; you know we'll figure that out. I just have to know that you're OK. Do you understand what you did was so reckless? Doing something like that, it's not like you … Is something else going on?"

I grew numb. I couldn't feel the words leaving my throat. I had to believe the murmured sound I was hearing. "Mum, I don't remember anything else."

How did she know? I knew this was a stupid thought; she was my mum, of course she'd sense when I wasn't myself. I began to worry she could read my thoughts, suddenly realising that I wasn't so good at keeping secrets from her. My poker face was starting to unpeel. I had to figure out another way – a better way – to prove to her things were OK. That I was OK.

I didn't want to talk about it anymore. I was slowly discovering the details and I didn't want to share them with her. I felt bad, but it was for the better.

I thought it was for the better.

Our conversation ended with her sigh. That simple sound cut me. She pushed herself off the sofa and wandered to the bathroom. I kept silent. My eyes followed her until she left my sight. I thought that maybe she was giving me time to try and remember, or she was leaving it to Dr Wilson. Maybe she'd managed to accept the fact that I might have been opening up to him during the therapy sessions. I did know that she was pleased I was still going to them.

I sat at the kitchen table. Mum asked me to write the shopping list. She told me she was grocery shopping as soon as she got home. I held the pen in my hand and wrote down what I wanted and other things I thought we needed. I twirled the pen around my fingers as I thought of other items. A feeling itched within me. I turned the page, and my hand began to draw lines with the black ink.

Surprisingly the act didn't feel foreign. It didn't feel like it had been months since I'd drawn. Months since I'd created. I continued to form lines and my thoughts remained muted. I traced over lines I'd already drawn and I felt a small grin on my face. But the overshadowing part of my mind realised what I was doing. I dropped the pen on the table and looked at the paper. Looked at the face I'd sketched. It looked like it was meant to be someone from my past. Someone who I shouldn't share a connection to. Someone I didn't want to remember. His strong jaw. His cold eyes. The beginning shape of his thick hair. I shook my head in a hope to remove the thoughts that hadn't yet formed. I ripped the page from the book, scrunched it up and threw it in the bin.

Curled on the sofa, resting my face on my palm with the TV on, I wasn't paying attention to the show. I was lost in a daydream.

My phone beeped. It was a text from Kai.

Kai: What are u doing at this very second?
Me: At home watching TV.
Kai: Do u want company?

Mum walked through the front door. "P, I'm home!"

I left the lounge, strolled up to her and kissed her on the cheek. "Hey Mum. How was your day?"

"Uh super busy … and I think I'm engaged."

"Um, what?"

"There's this sweet patient, he's in his early eighties, just had a hip replacement and he said to me yesterday, 'If I make it out of this operation and you're still single tomorrow, we'll get married.' So today, while another nurse and I checked up on him, he proposed and I accepted."

"Well, congratulations."

"Thanks P."

"When's the wedding?"

"I don't know; we haven't discussed dates. I think he's really into the proposing phase – he asked me three times. But I mean I must be something special. Get this: I was told he only flirted with *one* other nurse for the rest of today." Her laughter filled the room.

"So did anything else exciting happen or did being proposed to take up most of your day?"

"Well it's kind of hard to top once you've been proposed to. *But* on my way home this douchebag cut me off! He sped right up and went from the far right lane all the way over to the left. I *hate* when they do that!"

I smiled. She would never realise how much I missed her driving complaints. The way she just said things and apologised for them later – if she had to.

"And I don't really want to go food shopping tonight, but we *have* to have something in the cupboards other than those stale crackers. How was *your* day sweetheart? Everything been OK?"

"Yeah. Everything's fine. I feel all right. My day's been OK. Um Mum, can Kai come over?"

"P, what are you talking about? His car's parked outside. I thought he was already here."

What? He was texting me, asking if he could come over when he was already outside my house?

"P you don't have to ask permission to be alone with him in the house, you know my rules. I trust you, and Kai seems like a nice guy. Plus if he hurts you, I'll rip his balls off. Now, go fetch him. His car's turned off so the heater can't be on. We don't want to be blamed for the kid dying of pneumonia. Plus, we can't afford another lawsuit and, if it came to jail time, orange is *not* my colour."

I kissed her on the cheek again and made my way outside. The crisp cold attacked me from every angle. I wished I'd put a coat on. I marched straight to his car and thumped on the passenger's window. Kai was looking down at his phone, probably waiting for my response. "Hey! You! We don't want no stalking in this neighbourhood. So get out of here. You hear?" I laughed a little. My breath became fog. I opened the door and sat inside. It wasn't much warmer, but it beat standing in the cold.

"Oh my god! That scared the crap out of me." Kai gripped the clothing near his heart.

"What are you doing here, Kai? You text me asking if I want company but you're *already* sitting outside my house."

"I thought that if I knocked on your door and you saw me there you would feel obliged to say yes. This way, you can say no."

"But if I'd replied yes, you would've been at my door in a matter of seconds. Don't you think I would've asked how you got here so fast?"

"Well my plan was to either charm my way out of that question or convince you that I have superpowers."

"Oh, OK then. So, are you coming inside?"

"You haven't answered my question."

I frowned at him.

"Do you want company?"

"Yes."

"Then inside I shall go."

We jogged to the front door and entered the house. I was ready to defrost. The warmth of the heater began to thaw my limbs. I could breathe easier and my movements weren't as stiff.

"Hi Emma," Kai said.

"Hello Kai."

I thought of her threat to rip his balls off and giggled.

"So, what are your intentions with my daughter today then?"

The question seemed highly inappropriate. One false move on his behalf and he would no longer have his testicles.

"Well my intentions are just to keep her company. I'm predicting just a casual hang-out. Watch TV or maybe a movie while we dine on microwaveable popcorn."

"The popcorn might have to wait till I'm back from food shopping."

The three of us stood in the kitchen with different smiles on our faces.

"OK then. Mum, why don't *you* go shopping, bring us back the much-needed food and popcorn for the movie, and Kai and I will be in the lounge, hanging out."

I was happy Kai was there. He was a perfect example of me *getting back out there*. Proving to Mum I was fine. His presence was tangible evidence that I could use to fight my case with her, instead of just my words.

When Kai and I were home alone, a feeling of anxiousness spread through my system. We were in the lounge, plonked on the sofa at either end. I wondered if he wished one of us had chosen to sit a little closer to the other?

"So what are we watching? Or what have you been watching?" Kai asked.

"Just channel surfing really. Right now it's this *reality* show about rich bitches." I knew the show offered too many colours, but for some reason I found it easy to watch. I allowed myself to throw myself into their drama and focus on the problems of their lives for a short while.

"OK, give me the low down. What do I need to know?"

"All you really need to know is they're rich, some more than others, and the ones who are, *love* to rub that in every chance they get. There's always drama and they always over-react and fight about everything and call each other disgusting names, all while diamonds sparkle and they try to cover up how much plastic surgery they've actually had done."

"Do you often watch this sort of stuff?"

"Not really. Only if there's nothing else on and I have nothing better to do."

We watched the show together and laughed at the housewives' expense. I hid behind their commotion. Drowned myself in their world. Kai and I decided which rich bitches we liked and the ones who should donate all of their money to charity.

The show ended. We both fell silent. I suddenly thought of our third date and the way things had changed when I'd asked about his family and then the other day when he played me his song. His secret I still needed to decode.

I stared at him, half-expecting him to say, "Tell me something" but no words left his lips. *Was he reading me? What had he uncovered? What was he thinking?* So many questions, so many thoughts journeyed through my mind but there was one that constantly came back to me. One that I had asked myself many times since we went on our second date. "Can I ask you something?"

"Sure," Kai said.

"Not to sound self-centred, but you're the only person I know who knows about my car crash, who hasn't actually *asked* me about it. Why?"

"I just thought if you wanted to tell me, you would, 'cause you *can*. And I kind of don't think that's my place."

"What's not your place?"

"Your past."

I knitted my eyebrows.

Kai softly smiled. He shuffled closer to me. My insides fluttered but then my mind grew dark.

"What I mean is, what you want to tell me about your past is up to you. I would prefer no lies, though. You see, right now I'm part of your present, potentially part of your future. Maybe even your distant future. You don't need to tell me what you did in the past. It might sound mean, but I don't care."

"Oh ..."

Kai kept his sight on me. His brightness was almost overpowering.

I tried to halt the question building in my throat, but the words escaped. "Why do you like me?"

"Why wouldn't I?"

"No really, why do you like me?"

"You interest me ... You're creative, like me. I want to get to know you."

"But I'm nothing special."

"I think you are." Kai smiled.

"But,"

"Not to sound rude, but you can't tell me how I should feel about you. I feel how I feel. And I'm enjoying every second of getting to know you."

"Well, why can't I get to know you then?"

"What do you mean?"

"Did you not ask about my past so you're not obliged to tell me about *yours*?"

"No … If you want to know about my past all you have to do is ask."

"But I *did* ask you. I asked about your mum, your dad, if you had any siblings, just like you asked about mine; but you shot me down."

"I didn't shoot you down."

"Yes you did. You think *me* telling you about the crash was on my agenda for that day? I didn't *mean* to tell you; it just slipped out. And if I hadn't told you that day then you wouldn't even know about it right now. I didn't intend to tell you because I didn't, I *don't*, want your sympathy. I just don't understand why you didn't tell me about *your* family, when I openly spoke to you about mine, even my loser dad."

"Because it's kind of a difficult subject." Kai said.

"And you think me pouring my guts out to you every time we're together, telling you things about me, is *easy*? Well Kai, news flash, I've been through some shit." All of a sudden the memories played. They repeated over and over like they were glued to my senses. I couldn't shake them away. I tried to think of a dark place I could crawl into. A place they could crawl into. Somewhere for me to hide.

I rushed to stand and closed my eyes, then kept them shut tight. Tried to block the memories. I turned around and ran to the bathroom, locked the door and slid to the tiled floor. I tried to swallow my cries but the tears rolled anyway.

I heard Kai's footsteps coming towards the bathroom, but I didn't want him to see me like that. *He must've thought I was a freak.*

He gently knocked on the door. "Peyton …"

I bit my tongue.

"Peyton, are you OK? Do you need me to get you anything? Do you want me to call your mum?"

"No!" *No. Not my mum. She can't know. She thinks I'm finally free of the darkness. She thinks I'm fine.* "No. Thanks. I'm fine, Kai. I just … I'm fine." I knew he knew I wasn't. And somehow I knew he wouldn't let it rest.

Silence lingered. I felt him on the other side of the door.

My tears stopped falling. The flashes retreated back into their dungeon. I didn't know what I was supposed to say to make Kai forget about what had just happened. It probably didn't help that we were separated by a locked door. A part of me began to question if he was still there, or if my imagination was playing tricks on me. Because deep down I wanted him to be there. He didn't have to say anything. Just be.

"Kai?"

"Yeah?"

My heart melted.

I didn't say anything in response. I didn't know what to say.

"Peyton, you can tell me whatever you want. I know how that must sound after our little, well whatever happened just then, but you can tell me *anything*. I swear it won't leave my lips. I can help. I *want* to help."

I didn't want him to know. If he did, then he'd look at me differently. He wouldn't look at me with wonderment. He wouldn't light up when he saw me. He wouldn't like me. I decided to steal his words. "Maybe another time."

Chapter SEVENTEEN

I found comfort in Dr Wilson's office. The neutral tones were colours I was prepared for, colours I accepted, even though I still preferred grey. I placed myself on the edge of the chair. I was overflowing with despair.

Dr Wilson sat opposite me. "How are you feeling today, Peyton?"

The words almost didn't leave my mouth. They were wedged in my throat. "I'm OK. How are you?"

"I'm well thank you." He leant towards the coffee table and grabbed his notebook.

My breaths were shallow.

"I've actually got something to show you."

I didn't know what he was going to show me, but I was unprepared. I no longer wanted the neutral surroundings. I no longer wanted to acknowledge them. *I wanted my darkness.*

Dr Wilson flicked through several lined pages and stopped when he got to a certain page. "Ah, here it is ..." His grey eyes glanced to me then back to the paper then back to me.

"Peyton, before I show you this, I want you to have an open mind."

I glared at him and swallowed the lump in my throat. *He's sending me off to a madhouse. He thinks I'm insane. I knew I shouldn't have told him the truth. I shouldn't have taken a chance on him. Why did I do that?*

"Can you do that for me?" He asked. His voice soothing. Rich.

I found myself nodding. I didn't remember giving my head that command.

Dr Wilson shuffled to the edge of his cushioned chair. He stretched his arm towards me, offering his notebook. My eyes looked up at him. He nodded encouragingly. I reached out, my hand trembling slightly. I hoped he didn't notice. I grabbed the book and retreated in my chair. Wishing it would swallow me whole.

Looking down at the paper I saw a drawing. An inked sketch of a couple. The male and female figures had their backs turned as if they were walking away. They were dressed in winter clothes from the 1940s – hats, coats and gloves. Confused, my eyes remained on the drawing.

"Now I know it's pretty rough, but what do you think?"

"You …" I cleared my throat. "You drew this?"

Dr Wilson sighed. "Yeah …" He licked his lips. "What are your thoughts?"

I took a breath. "It's not too bad."

"Come on, be honest Peyton. I can take it."

I gazed down at the paper and scanned the sketch's faults.

"Well, I mean apart from the proportions being a little off, it's pretty good. Drawn quite well. It's obviously two human figures." I still felt unsure. Like I was unable to fully grasp what was happening in that moment. I offered his notebook back. He took it from me. I took another deep breath. *So he wasn't sending me off to a madhouse?*

"You draw then?"

"Not as much as I used to. Back in the day, I was always sketching or doodling on scrap bits of paper. When I was younger I actually got into graffiti."

I snickered.

"Well, you may not think it now, but I was a cool kid, Peyton. Believe it or not, I was almost a high-school dropout. A couple of my mates and I stayed out late and tagged walls. I got hooked on designing. I did loads of artwork for my friends' skateboard decks. Then I moved on to cartooning. Through my art I got to know some kids that weren't well off, they had family problems, some even lived on the streets, and I wanted to find a way to help them. So I did some volunteering at shelters and community groups then found myself studying counselling. Drawing is now more of an occasional hobby ... But I would have *loved* to have an art space like the one you have."

I was quite impressed. I would never have pegged Dr Wilson as an artist. But his desire to help others was no surprise. The thought of art – my art, or lack thereof – reminded me of why I was so sad. It all hit me. I couldn't help myself. I sobbed.

"Peyton, what's the matter?" Dr Wilson stretched to a side table and cautiously handed me several tissues.

I tried to speak but I had difficulty getting oxygen into my lungs. The tears fell into my open mouth and I tasted their salt. Words stuck in my throat. *I thought that that must have been how it felt to really cry. I knew why it felt so familiar.*

"Take your time, Peyton … Just breathe." His smooth voice guided me through.

Once the words came, I couldn't stop them. "Because of what happened to me, I have this darkness and I try to run from it. The haunting feeling strikes me like a whip and I can't shake it away. I *can't* shake it. I try … I try my *hardest* to ignore it. To ignore it all. I don't want to remember the details. But the harder I push it away, the stronger it returns and I dread the moment when I can't bury it anymore. When I'm *forced* to remember. I try to keep it in. I don't want it to see the light. It's easier to hide things in shadows."

After my confession I cried another river of tears.

"Peyton, it's natural, after what you've been through, to feel lost. But casting yourself into what you call your darkness and shadows sounds like you're pushing yourself away, like you're pushing your feelings away and therefore you could be pushing away the people who can help you the most."

"But I don't want them to know … What would my mum think? My brother would probably kill him. And I … I don't want to remember. I don't want to relive it."

"Sometimes, to get past certain moments in our lives, the only way is through."

The rest of the session was formed with a mixture of me crying and trying to listen to Dr Wilson. His voice. His words. I needed him to anchor me back to some form of stability. I needed his kindness. His advice to help me with my fight. But I knew what he said wouldn't change my past. It couldn't change my past.

Any of it.

Chapter EIGHTEEN

For the third day in a row, Kai invited himself over to my house. I think he felt some sort of responsibility, because he was the only one – other than myself and Dr Wilson – who knew I wasn't stable. They were the only ones who had seen me break down.

There he was. I didn't want him to be. But for some reason I couldn't turn him away. There was a lure about him. Something that seemed to make it OK that he was near. Half of me wanted him to be there and the other half needed him to leave. The fact that Kai kept coming around to see me made my brain twist with thoughts. I naturally latched onto the idea that he was another person I had to convince I was OK.

His presence was bright but his eyes were weary. I knew he had questions. I also knew he wouldn't push me for answers. What happened before, when I locked myself in the bathroom, was part of my past. And he said he didn't care what I did in my past. I wondered if his personal philosophy would change if he were present in that part of my past. I wondered if because he was there – caught up in my breakdown – he now had a right to ask me what was going on.

Underneath it all, I felt like I was no longer the girl who intrigued him. I was no longer a girl he would be interested in. *How could someone like me or want me, if they knew what had happened to me?* I couldn't help but feel that I was just a charity case. That he just had a need to check up on me and make sure I was still alive, and that need would slowly dwindle when he found a different way to help me. I was worried that that might include telling my mum.

Kai and I settled on the sofa. I wanted a distance between us. I didn't want him close to me. Not then. The TV was on but I didn't know what was playing. I felt like I had just created another armoured wall that Kai would have to climb. But that wall wasn't just for my want to be strong in front of him or for my protection, but for his. I looked into his luminous eyes. They were beautiful. They could've outshone my pessimism – if I'd let them. *I wondered when the day would come that I wouldn't see them anymore.*

"You know, usually when people first meet me they ask if I'm wearing contacts." Vacantly, I searched his face. "No contacts over here, baby."

I smiled weakly. His attempt to lighten the mood and make me happy simply drowned in the haze of my grey state.

"When I was younger, my mum told me that people with

one blue eye and one brown eye can look upon heaven *and* earth."

My heart lifted slightly at the mention of his mum. He'd never brought her up before. I hadn't mentioned her or his family since our quarrel. I wanted to give him time. *I wanted him to trust me.* I wanted to know about her. I wanted to know about him.

"Tell me what you see."

Kai smiled. "Well, in heaven I've found a pretty awesome spot for just the two of us. There's enough space around for both our families, but that little spot is just for you and me. And here on earth I see *so* much that I want to explore. So many adventures. So many new experiences."

His smile was bright – it was almost a glare. I wanted to find a dimming switch. That part of me was wary about letting light in. The other part of me wanted the light to reign – let myself soak in his colours. The colours I secretly missed. They were like the colours I used to splatter and bead on my canvases. The colours I used to blend over hot press paper. I liked the way he saw the world. Everything in technicolour.

My thoughts drifted to the drive home from hospital and being thankful for the grey day, knowing I wasn't ready for colour. *I still didn't feel ready for it.* Sometimes when I thought about it too much, I realised that without Kai around my world was boring and grey and I tried to paint it darker because I still needed the shadows to hide in. Deep down I knew having Kai around was helping me. Changing me. His unique perspective was helping me grow courage. Making me think that one day I could be more than OK.

A sudden urge came over me. My stomach twisted. I ignored my doubtful whisperings. I rose from the sofa, grabbed Kai's hand and tugged at his arm. "Come with me."

"Where are we going?"

I didn't answer. He'd know soon enough.

We drifted through my house in silence. I stopped us in front of the door. I released his hand, even though a part of me didn't want to.

"This is the inside entrance to my Art Cave."

It was where my secret was hidden.

"Just like with your songs, I put hidden messages and my secrets in my work. That's why I don't want to go in there … There's something in there that reflects the dark in me. Something I'm trying to hide from. It will make me remember my crash and everything else. I guess I'm scared. Afraid. I don't think I'm ready for it … I don't want to be ready for it."

Kai viewed the cream painted door. His eyes travelled up and down as if he could see through the wood. I clenched at the thought of him seeing inside. He gently took my hand in his.

Both staring at the door, I was relieved he didn't ask me if we were going in, even though I knew he wanted to. He was giving me time. Space. He was giving me what I needed. He was just being there. And for me, at that time, it was enough.

We remained at the door. Our hands still locked. I grew fidgety.

"Lunch?" he asked.

A week later my therapy session felt like a welcome part of my week. It might not be what I wanted, but it was what I needed.

It felt different as I stepped into the office – into the next hour of my life. I had come to realisation that Dr Wilson knew of my past yet he treated me no differently. That thought made me consider telling Mum, but my body shuddered at the thought.

As I made my way to a seat, my eyes lingered over the table, hoping to see a drawing, a doodle. I wanted to see something new. He was one of few people who truly knew how much art was my passion and how much I was missing it. At times, I wasn't entirely prepared to accept the fact that he was someone I could relate to.

I sank into my usual cushioned chair. Dr Wilson leant back opposite me. His ankle rested on his knee. His eyes were mesmerising. I immediately wanted to draw and paint them. I hadn't really thought about drawing something new until he'd showed me his sketch. "How are you today, Peyton?"

"I'm fine. How are you?"

"I'm doing very well, thank you."

"I went to my Art Cave. That boy came round and I showed him. Just the door. We didn't go in. But he knows where it is now. He knows that's where I keep my dark side.

Where it hides. Where I keep my secret. He's the only person who's been near the door. Near my art. Near that darkness."

"And how does that make you feel?"

I bit my lip and let it slide through my teeth. "OK. I think … There's something about him I can trust. And that makes me feel both happy and scared."

"That's a big a step you took, Peyton, letting someone else near a personal space. You should be very proud of yourself. It doesn't matter that you didn't go in, the fact that you were brave enough to share that moment with someone is a great step."

I nodded, a little longer than any sane – stable – person would. Maybe the motion of moving my head had become a natural impulse. Something my body knew it needed to do to ward off the demons.

"Dr Wilson?"

"Yes?"

"Do you think …" I bit my tongued. Paused my thoughts. "Never mind."

"Peyton, I can't even imagine how you're feeling. What you've experienced is something life changing and everybody deals with it differently. Don't think for a second that what you're feeling is wrong. That's how *you're* feeling. Please know that what you wanted to ask me right then, you can. You can say anything in here. Believe me when I tell you this is a safe place. Your safe place."

Tears dripped. My lips quivered. "Who's going to want me? Who's going to be able to look past what I can't even bear to think about?" I set my blurry sight to the ceiling. "I'm scared that I'll always be alone. That because I'm pushing my thoughts and my feelings away, that I'll keep stopping myself from allowing something good to happen to me. Because it feels wrong to let happiness in. It doesn't feel safe to let the light in because what if it shines too brightly and it uncovers everything about that day? If I can't even bear to look at myself, then why should someone else?"

"It might seem hard to believe, but people can surprise you. Even yourself."

I cleared my throat. I couldn't deal with this right now. I needed a subject change. "Have you been sketching?"

"I have actually."

A part of me felt lighter. I wanted to see what else he had produced. I wanted to keep my mind from my art. From my thoughts.

Dr Wilson flicked through the same notebook and stopped on a page. He leant towards me and handed me the book. I took it, and looked at the drawing.

"How's this one?" He said. "You can be honest. Like I said before, I can take it."

My eyes trailed the image. "Um ... Dr Wilson ... this is ... unique."

"And?"

"Kind of *terrible* actually. Nothing like the other one you showed me. I mean,"

"Go on."

"Well ... I know art is expression, and if you were going

for the concept that a four-year-old drew it, then you succeeded."

"Ouch. I expected you to be a little less harsh." He grinned.

"Well this is therapy. Isn't this where you're supposed to let your demons out?" I rolled my lips then looked at his drawing. I tilted my head. "What's it supposed to be, anyway?"

"Tell me what *you* see. You're the better artist after all."

"How can you say that? You haven't even seen my art."

"I don't doubt your art skills, Peyton. I can tell it's something you're greatly passionate about. And when the time is right you'll be back in your Art Cave creating again. Well then, art critic, tell me what you see."

I looked at his creation. "I see a young girl's face. Her eyes are a little skew-whiff, which could represent two points of view or an imbalance in her life. Her hair's all over place, which clearly represents her wild nature *or* potential madness. She has a wide smile that shows her willingness to continue. Her willingness for adventure." I quickly handed his notebook back to him. The description sounded too familiar.

"Wow … I didn't know it said all that."

"It's all in the eye of the beholder. Obviously it means something different to you."

Dr Wilson chuckled. His smile grew. "It's an impromptu sketch of my niece. She's a wild child. Full of energy." He turned the page of his notebook. "I've never been good at drawing facial features, unless they're cartoonish. I can never make them look realistic. I've tried but I can never get them right."

The air suddenly shifted, altering the mood. Somehow, I knew his next words were going to be more serious than him asking me to critique his drawing.

"Do you believe you'll be ready to go into your Art Cave one day?"

My heart slowly thumped. I took a breath. "I have to believe. If I don't, I know I'll get lost in the dark and then I'll be forced to fight this battle with myself forever, and I know that I won't win that war."

Chapter NINETEEN

The next day Kai arrived at my house. I opened the door. There he was. A diverted smile on his face. His watery eyes were barely open and the skin around them was red. He stretched out his hand. "These are for you."

I took the bouquet of flowers and admired their bright beauty. "Kai, what's wrong with your face?"

"Um … I'm allergic to flowers." He sneezed.

"Oh my god. Get inside and wash your face!"

As Kai washed his face in the bathroom, I arranged the flowers in a vase and left them on the kitchen table. I sat awkwardly in the lounge, hoping he was OK and wondered why he'd do such a thing.

A couple of minutes passed.

With a fresh face, Kai walked into the room, with his guitar in his hand. I hadn't even noticed he'd brought it with him because of the commotion with the flowers.

"Are you OK?"

"Yeah, I'm fine." Kai smiled.

"Why did you do that?"

"I wanted to bring you flowers."

"But you're *allergic* to them."

"I wanted you to have them."

"Thank you. They're really nice. And that was really sweet, but *please* don't do that again. It looked like your face was melting off or something."

Kai chuckled. His mop of hair almost covered his eyes. I wanted to sweep it from his face just so I could see them. But he flicked it so I didn't have to. My body tingled at his warm colours, like a tropic sunset. Part of me wanted him to come closer. Wanted him to lean in to me and kiss me. Suddenly, I felt unsure. Questioned if I should be feeling this slight temptation.

"So Peyton, are you ready for this guitar lesson?"

Kai and I had messaged a few times over the days. He wanted to teach me something he knew that I didn't. I mentioned I'd never played guitar and I'd always wanted to learn.

"I guess I'm ready."

"I'll have you playing like the best of the best in no time. Then we can start up a world-famous band. Obviously we'll have to do auditions to find our other members. Unless you just want to be a duo …"

"Well Liam can play the drums. Actually he and his friends used to come around and jam. And I know a little on the drums, too."

"Oh, that's cool. We should keep them in mind."

Kai and I spent the morning playing guitar. My mind was distracted by thoughts I tried to ignore. I wondered what Dr Wilson thought about me. I wondered what he wrote in his notebook. Most of the time he just listened to me. It was rare for me to see him write something. Which was why I always wanted to know what it was when he did. During our sessions, sometimes he'd draw. Doodle, actually. I watched as he twisted his pen over the paper. My intrigue grew. He never showed me those small sketches and when I left the therapy room, a burning desire pulsed through me. A desire to create. On the drive home, after Mum had picked me up, I'd loosely latch onto that desire. My thoughts gleamed with what to draw or paint. My heart beat with trivial excitement. But by the time we pulled into the driveway and I stepped inside, the desire fled.

During the guitar lesson I strummed at the strings and listened to Kai's kind instructions, but my heart wasn't in it. I knew Kai noticed there was something wrong with me; he stopped his teaching and just strummed it himself. I liked the sound. He played a little tune. I wondered if it was an original. I wondered if there were words that went with it. It was nice to hear the chords waver through the air, instead of silence. That was the usual sound – along with the ticking of the clock – I heard when I was home alone, unless the TV was on – and I would only put that on to soothe my thoughts and distract my mind. These days I hardly played music. Only when I needed to drown my sorrows – myself. I wasn't prepared for all of the feelings music could bring.

I wasn't ready for those colours.

A part of me wanted to tell Kai something, so he didn't leave thinking I was a complete freak or a waste of time. I felt that maybe he thought I was playing with him – but I wasn't – that's just how I was. That was just how I felt. Scared. Grey. Stuck.

"Tell me something, Peyton Swift. Something new …"

I glanced at him. It's like he'd read my thoughts. I silently debated my response as we sat on the carpet. Kai leant against the sofa and continued to strum his guitar. He looked so comfortable there, like he was making himself at home. I kind of liked that.

I took a deep breath. "I've been going to therapy." My brain registered the words after I spoke them. I had debated on telling him this, but thought every part of me had agreed not to speak it. "Sorry …"

"Why are you sorry?"

"Well it's not something you say in casual conversation."

"You already know you can tell me anything, Peyton. Do you want to talk about it?"

"I've only been going since the car crash." I rushed my words, trying to prove to him I wasn't a freak. A small part of me was ashamed for seeing a therapist. Sometimes just the mere thought of it made me feel uncomfortable. Especially now Dr Wilson knew my darkest secret. Almost every part of me hoped Kai still liked me. "I just talk about things to do with that."

I stopped talking. My heart beat fast within my chest. *Was he judging me? Did he think I was weird?* My eyes searched the lounge and landed on the TV remote. *Should I turn the TV on? Make him forget about what I had just told him?*

Kai continued to strum the strings. The tune slightly changed. It felt a little more relaxed. I couldn't stop myself. I looked at him. He smiled at me. I felt numb inside. I couldn't feel my body trembling, but I knew it was.

What was he thinking?

"Therapy isn't something to be ashamed about. It's good that you're going. Sometimes it's needed."

I sighed. The numbness dissolved as my heart rushed beats. My blood felt as though it was shooting through my veins. I smiled the best I could.

Kai and I stayed in the lounge together before he went to work. For me, the minutes felt unnatural. I kind of wished that he wouldn't stay for as long as he did. But as soon as he left a part of me missed his warms colours and the gentleness he fuels. The way he finds home – comfort – wherever he is. I found myself thinking about the way his radiance flourishes when he speaks, smiles and moves. I'd never seen anything like it.

Later that day Liam messaged me. I was happy to hear from him. I liked that he was so far away. It felt like I wasn't keeping my secret from him too. At least it was easier to pretend with the distance between us.

Liam: Hey P what's going on? Study is boring me so I thought I'd speak to one of my favourite people.

Me: How many people didn't respond until u got to me??

Liam: Ouch!! P u know ur number two.

Me: 2?!?!

Liam: Well Mum has to be number one!!

Me: Aww mama's boy.

Liam: Shut up!

Me: U can't tell me to shut up Liam. I am keeping ur almost expulsion from our mummy.

Liam: I take it back … Have u thought any more of the reward u want from me for doing so?

Me: Actually that hasn't really been on my mind.

Liam: What has?

Me: I told Kai I've been going to therapy. He seemed cool with it. But I can't help but still feel worried.

Liam: If he starts being stupid about it & treats u differently then he's not worth your time. You've gotta be with someone who likes u for u. & you're amazing P. Don't let anyone tell u otherwise!

I began texting a response when Liam sent another message.

Liam: & when will I be seeing more drawings? I check my inbox every day hoping for an attachment.

I knew he was exaggerating, but I smiled at the thought of him wanting to see more of my art.

Liam: Am I gonna have to break into ur art cave to see something?

No. He couldn't do that.

Me: Give it a little time. I'll send u something soon! X
Liam: I hope that's a promise!
Me: I promise.
Liam: Well I'll speak to u soon. I better get back to this assignment. xx
Me: Has somebody better on ur favourite people list just texted u?
Liam: There is nobody better/more important than my top 2! Xx
Me: LOL! Speak soon X

Later that night I curled up in my bed, wrapped my blankets around me and pretended nothing could hurt me. No nightmares could touch me. But as soon as I closed my eyes and tried my descent into sleep, my phone beeped.

It was a text from Kai. Worried, I picked up the phone.

Kai: Dream a little dream of me, Peyton Swift.

I'd try. And I would. I didn't want to have those nightmares again.

Chapter TWENTY

Kai and I were in the kitchen. His hair was tied in a loose bun. Ever since I'd met him it seemed as though he'd been trying out different styles – but everything suited him.

He rubbed his hands together. "So, what are we making for lunch? I'm starving."

Kai and I moved around the kitchen as we prepared a meal. I instructed him on where to find the correct utensils and saucepans, and together we chopped vegetables, boiled water, heated sauce and cooked pasta. As I stirred the sauce, the bright colours of the vegetables overwhelmed me. I glanced at Kai, to find him already staring at me. Quickly averting my attention back to the cooking food, I felt trapped between colours. It was impossible not to recognise that my and Kai's natural chemistry mirrored the brightness of the food in the saucepans.

"Do you wanna hear a joke?" Kai asked.

I shyly looked at him. "OK then."

"A mushroom walks into a bar, the bartender says, 'Hey,

you can't drink here.' Mushroom says, 'Why not, I'm a Fun-gi!'"

A smile spread across my face.

"Did you like that one?"

"It wasn't too bad."

"Do you want another?"

I nodded. "Go on then."

"What do you call a fake noodle?"

I softly shook my head. "I don't know."

"An impasta!"

"Those jokes are so lame!" I laughed. The sound escaped as if it were natural. It felt good to release that energy.

This was the way I used to be. I wanted to be like this more. I wanted to feel this more. There were times throughout the day, too many to count, when I question myself, analyse my actions and thought patterns. What happened to me changed me so drastically. And now I wondered whether it was OK for me to be happy. Content. Was it wrong to let myself go?

Right now, Kai was the only one in my life who I could almost be my old self with. His presence rang with safety and I wanted that around. He was no longer just a distraction or a replacement for my self-inflicted pain. He was becoming more.

I stopped myself thinking about the acceptance of light. I shut my happiness off. Crawled back into my shell and huddled behind my armoured walls.

"It's OK to laugh, you know," Kai said.

I didn't know if that was true. I didn't even fathom a response. I was uncertain whether it was OK for me to laugh. Whether it was OK for me to feel cheerful. I was still unprepared to risk it.

I focused on the food. Turned off the stove and began to dish out our lunch. We ate with a side of controlled conversation. It was my fault things between us were slightly awkward. I had pushed him away because of the darkness I craved. It seemed Kai didn't care – about any of it. He seemed to be built of patience.

Maybe he didn't think I was a freak.

Our empty bowls were in front of us. Still the air stirred with the rich smell of tomato, garlic and parmesan cheese. Kai's eyes appeared locked on me. Something itching at his chest. Burning at his throat. I opened my mouth, about to ask if he was OK, but before I could, he began to talk.

"I know you want to know about my family … And if it's OK with you, I'd like to tell you now."

I nodded. I hadn't expected it to happen that day, but if he was ready to share it with me, I had to be ready to listen.

"There's no easy way to say any of this, so I'm just going to speak it the best way I can."

I braced myself. *Was it really what I wanted?* I was ill equipped.

Kai took a breath then licked his lips. "Um, so … I grew up in an abusive household. I watched my dad beat my mum from before I learnt to walk. He drank too much too often.

He let his frustrations out on my mum whenever he felt like it."

My heart slowed. I felt sympathy rise to the surface as if it were about to ooze out of my pores. I sensed it growing in my eyes. I hoped he hadn't noticed. He probably wouldn't want it. Just like I didn't want it from him.

"I was about five when he hit me the first time. I remember waking up to bruises that hurt even before I moved. Mum wasn't home when it happened, and later that night she found out. I remember them getting into a fight about it, a screaming match. I lay in bed covering my ears. I shut my eyes tight and tried to pretend I was somewhere else. The next morning I saw her with a swollen black eye. I felt like it was my fault and I didn't know how to make it better.

"Mum would always put on a brave face when she was in front of me. Her smile was the only thing that made me feel safe. When I was about eight, she tried to leave him. She packed a suitcase and we went to this motel, but somehow he found us. I don't remember how it happened, but we went back home … I hated it there. I hated my dad and what he did to us. What he did to Mum."

I never thought Kai was perfect, but seeing his colours somewhat fading right in front of me, showed just how much of an impact his childhood had on him and the type of person he was because of it. Somehow he'd made light of his situation. He'd kept colour in his world. I held onto the thin hope that maybe, one day, I could too.

"A few months later, Mum told me I was going to be

a big brother. I remember feeling worried for how things would change when the baby arrived. How my dad would be … But Mum was the happiest I'd seen her in a long time. When I saw that something was growing inside her, I became excited too. I'd help rub that gel stuff on her stomach to stop her getting stretch marks, and I was filled with more joy each time I felt the baby kick. Mum took my hand and placed it in the exact spot it needed to be and I would pretend I was an explorer finding the best treasure there was. As the months passed I couldn't wait to meet the baby. She told me it was a girl. I decided I was going to be better than my dad. I wanted to always keep her safe. Be there whenever she needed me. I already loved her and I hadn't even met her."

I watched as Kai lit up. It wasn't the brightest I'd ever seen him. His colours weren't solid. But it was the first time – other than when he spoke about the way he felt about his mum – that he'd shown a spark of happiness. His baby sister must have brought magic to their lives. I wanted to meet her. I wanted to see if she was colourful too.

Kai lent back on the wooden chair, but not in a carefree, cool-guy kind of way. He was stiff. Almost like a deer in headlights. Was he worried about what I was thinking? Did he think this would change the way I saw him?

He took a breath and released himself back into his story. His darkness.

"Every night, Dad went out drinking. Mum and I were home alone one night. I was at my happiest when it was just her and me. We used to play imagination games, like creating shapes with clouds or making up one-word-at-a-time stories in alphabetical order. We never really had much when I was growing up. This one night she bought us a huge box of chocolates. We stuffed our faces with them and couldn't stop laughing. It was one of the best nights I'd ever had. She put me to bed and I remember falling to sleep with a smile on my face.

"A loud thumping sound woke me up. It was still dark. I heard Mum screaming, crying. She was begging and Dad was just shouting at her. I jumped out of bed and ran to their room. She was lying on the floor, her face soaked with tears. Dad towered over her but he couldn't stand still, his body swaying. He stank of cigarettes and alcohol. I remember almost vomiting. I ran to Mum. A pool of blood was spreading over the floor. I didn't know what to do. Dad started to panic and rolled off excuses. It was like he was speaking to the walls. Mum whispered to me and I ran out of the room and followed her instructions. Minutes later the ambulance showed up and she was rushed to hospital…"

I listened to every word Kai said and immediately thought the worst. I saw the hurt painted on his face. The hurt I had never expected him to have. When I was around him, he had always been full of colour. *Was he decoding his song?*

"Mum lost the baby. My unborn sister had no chance of survival. I felt sick to my stomach knowing that I couldn't protect her or Mum. It happened during autumn. For a long time autumn just reminded me of death. When Mum was allowed to leave the hospital she packed another bag and that time we left for good.

"It took a little while, but we found a place of our own, we found our feet. A few years later Mum met a new man. He was so different to my dad; he was kind and caring. She married him and shortly after my little brother and sister were born. It was a new feeling. There was love and genuine happiness. No yelling. No pain. I felt safe. And where we live is a home not a house. I'd never known that before. It was something I thought didn't exist.

"A few years ago, my dad came round to our house. It had been about six years since I'd seen him or spoken to him. I don't know how he found us, but he rang the bell. I answered it and he was just there on our doorstep, as if he had a right to be. Straight away I told him to leave. Told him I'd call the police if he breathed in a way I didn't want him to. He tried to speak with me, but all the rage and all the hate I'd carried for him rose to the surface. He said he wanted me and Mum to come back; said that he'd changed and become a better man. I didn't believe him for a second. He touched my arm and I flung him back. Suddenly, he snapped. He became the man I remembered.

"He started telling me how worthless I was, how I was going to end up just like him. His face was so close to mine. I was waiting to for the stench of alcohol, but it never came. I felt my whole body tense. I pushed him away and told him to get off our property. He took a swing at me, but I dodged it. I clenched my fists and did what I had wanted to do for the longest time. I punched him in the face as hard as I could. He fell to the ground. I'll never forget the shock on his face. I clutched at his clothes, dragged him up and escorted him to the footpath. Reminded him to *never* come near Mum, my family, this house, or me ever again. We haven't seen or heard from him since.

"When I was just a kid, I promised myself that I would *never* be like him. I would be a better person, a better man. And If I ever had children, I would be a better father – someone my kids would be proud of. That's probably one of my biggest fears: me ending up like him."

"I'm so sorry you had to go through that. I never would've imagined …"

"You couldn't have known, Peyton. I usually try and dodge the subject. I'm not embarrassed of my mum or the great family I have now. I love my step dad and his son and my little brother and sister. That day you told me how your dad ditched you when you were young it made me realise it was another thing we have in common. And the way you spoke about your mum, how strong she is and how much you love her, it was like you were describing my mum and the way I feel about her. I just hate thinking about my dad and the things he did, the person he is. The things I had to see … I've never gone into that much detail with anyone before. You're really easy to talk to. Thanks for listening."

"Don't ever worry that you'll be like your dad. You're nothing like him."

"I like to think I'm nothing like him. But sometimes when I look in the mirror he's all I see."

"You're a better person, Kai. You have so much good in you."

"When I was younger, after my baby sister died, to help me and Mum get through things I would keep my left eye closed for as long as I could and only look at the world through my right eye, because that's the eye I could see heaven with. The place she is. I'd tell Mum that she was OK. That she was safe. That she was waiting for us. I know that probably sounds stupid, but I still do it every so often."

I grinned. "That's not stupid."

My heart warmed knowing that he seemed to trust me. I never imagined that he would have been through something like that and still be a person who was so full of light. I wanted to know what Kai was like when he was a kid. It seemed he'd always seen the world through different eyes.

Chapter TWENTY-ONE

I knew Dr Wilson was ready for me because there were two full boxes of tissues on the table. I was almost inclined to reach for a couple just in case, but I didn't think I would be crying that day.

"How are you today, Peyton?" Dr Wilson asked. His grey eyes were still magical.

"I'm OK. How are you?"

"I'm very good, thank you."

I wanted him to read me something, anything, just so I could hear his voice instead of mine. But this hour was mine.

"So the boy I met shared something really personal with me the other day and now it makes me feel like I should share something with him … I *want* to. At least I think I do … I mean, I already *have*. I told him about these therapy sessions, even though I'm embarrassed about them. I know I shouldn't be though. I was worried he would like me less. But we're still hanging out." I pulled at my sleeve. Rolled my lips. "There's something I could share with him and sometimes I think maybe I should. He knows I'm into art and he's said he wants to see some of my work. But I haven't got around to showing him anything. I kind of keep dodging that subject, because part of me is still unsure."

I could tell Dr Wilson was about to speak. But words escaped my mouth. "Sometimes I think it's best if I show him my art. You see, words are *his* thing. And I know he knows drawing and painting is mine, but sometimes I believe he might think a picture isn't enough, especially after what he just shared with me … Or, if I *tell* him about that certain moment, then we won't be the same. And I don't want him to look at me differently. I don't know if I could handle that. Not from him … I'm trying to believe that he won't judge me, but I don't want to take that chance and then never see him again. I think if I tell him what happened, he won't want to get to know me more or be with me."

"What happened to you before, Peyton, when you were …"

"I don't want you to say the word."

"Sorry, I don't want to make you uncomfortable. I know you said you don't want to relive the experience and that you want to forget. But what I wanted to ask was if you had remembered anything more?"

"There are some things I remember …"

"Would you feel comfortable telling me? Maybe if you tell me it might be easier to tell this boy. Or show him that artwork."

It wasn't that I didn't like Dr Wilson. It was just a risk

I was still unprepared to take. When I thought about what had happened to me for too long, I would feel like I was drowning. I knew the sessions were confidential and he hadn't told anyone about my past. But I had to latch onto an idea to convince myself not to share more details with him. I knew if I told Kai he'd keep my secret. He promised he would. But there was also the chance he'd never want to look at me again. Maybe the day of me not seeing his beautiful eyes was coming much faster than I expected.

"I don't know if I can tell you. I mean, I *know* I can but …"

"But you're not ready."

"No."

"And that's fine, Peyton. Talking about your true feelings is a difficult thing. And when you're ready to talk, I'm right here."

Would I ever be ready to talk?

The next few days I was at home. Lonely. Before the accident I would just spend the day in my Art Cave and create. I'd play music and stare at the empty pages and canvases, wondering what I would ink upon them. The music would enter my ears and spread through my veins, directing me towards a chromatic creation. I'd gently tip the page or canvas so the watercolours would bead. My fascination always lay with people. Their faces, profiles, smiles and eyes. I wanted to know what they were hiding. I loved intertwining the flow of the paint to create a story in their hair. Layer their eyes, blending my own thoughts, feelings and stories into the piece. The genre I played usually had an impact on the outcome – the colours I'd used, the strength of the lines, the secret I'd conceal – and I liked that. But since I hadn't even stepped inside my Art Cave, I was bound to my room, the lounge and the kitchen. I didn't want to spend more time in my room than I had to, because that was the place where I had the nightmares about my past. The darkness I was trying to keep hidden from Mum, Liam. Everyone.

Recently Kai hadn't been round much. He'd been given extra shifts and took them to help fill his bank account. Things grew grey when he wasn't with me, and I found myself trying to keep things dark. Every time I tried to see a colour, it felt forced. For some reason Kai was the only one who could make me believe that the colours I saw were genuine. Valid.

He and I spent the days texting. I enjoyed seeing his name displayed on my screen.

Kai: Done any drawing?

Me: No.

Kai: Do u plan to anytime soon?

Me: I'm not sure.

Kai: Well please remember I'm first in line for the substitute of Liam. I don't see anyone else fighting for that title … Is there anyone else?

Me: No.

The next morning, for some strange reason I grabbed my

iPod and made my way to the lounge. The battery had almost run out. I smiled as I scrolled through the list of songs, thinking back to the simple notion of when I could play a tune and it echoed my mood. I remembered when I allowed myself to feel. When I'd soak in colours like a sponge and seek out inspiration. Now I wouldn't even crack open an art book or set foot in my Art Cave, and I pushed my feelings aside. But they crept to the surface. Deep down I knew I couldn't keep this fight up forever. This battle was hanging over me like a noose.

My finger hovered over a song. A three-and-a-half-minute memory that once had held the power to soothe me. I knew I could let it do that again. Suddenly, my phone beeped.

Kai: Why haven't u been to the coffee shop lately? Lost the use of ur legs?

Me: No. I just haven't been there.

Me: Are u at work now?

Kai: Yeah. Meet me at our picnic table in 30 mins. I'll bring the hot chocolates with marshmallows.

Me: I'll bring the blanket.

On his lunch break, we sat at our picnic table and spoke about whatever we wanted. Just normal things, like the weather and what our days were like in a general sense.

We spoke a little more about his past, his childhood and some of his fonder memories. It wasn't hard to imagine Kai when he was younger, and how he took sheets from a cupboard and flung them on the grass and over a tree branch to create a tent and then he'd get lost in his own world. A place where he was always content with his pure imagination.

Later that day I was helping Mum prepare dinner. I wasn't hungry, but for some reason I found myself wishing that the deep breaths I was committedly drawing – taking in the sizzling vegetables and the Teriyaki sauce – would make my stomach rumble and Mum would hear it and then that could be used as more proof that I was OK.

I found myself disappointed. My stomach rumbles were only whispers. It was like my body was betraying me. Maybe because deep down I knew the rumbling of my stomach was no way to convince Mum I was all right.

Mum seemed to be more herself around me these past few days. Telling me about her driving stories after she got home from a long day at work – all of which included her driver's-tongue cuss words. We watched TV and the anxiousness I would feel about not knowing when she was going to ask me about my accident seemed to minimise. She hadn't asked me about it in a little while. But I still felt my guard was up.

As Mum tossed the noodles in the wok, my phone beeped. I stepped to the counter where it was and read the message.

Kai: I see green and gold. White, grey and black. Shapes take a hold and the sounds attack. I see pink and purple and all things blue. But nothing compares when I look at you.

I didn't know if it was an original poem. But it felt like him. It sounded like him. I didn't know to respond to such sweet words so I left it alone for a little while.

Later that night I decided to try and write my own little poem.

Me: Roses are red. Violets are blue. I really am lucky to have found someone like you.

Chapter TWENTY-TWO

I woke from a dreamless sleep. A nightmare-free sleep. For a moment I could pretend that the haunting had finished. That it had left. Right then, I decided I was going to enjoy the partial light.

I spent the morning with Mum until she had to leave for work. Liam called, and the three of us spoke for a little while. Mum and I sat at the kitchen table. We put the phone on loudspeaker so it was like he was there with us. I liked hearing about his day, his week. Hearing about his time in college. I smiled to myself, knowing Mum didn't know the half it. We kept it from her to protect her. What she didn't know wouldn't hurt her. A sinking feeling rested in my stomach, because those were the same reasons I repeated to convince myself not to share my deepest secret, too. I shook the thoughts from my mind.

Hearing Liam's voice made me miss him. Made me miss seeing him every day. I wanted him home so I could have some normality back in my life. Even though he had been at college a year before the incident and my accident I believed that if he came home, I would feel better. Because the last time I remembered feeling happy – really happy – was when the three of us were under one roof. It wasn't Liam's fault I felt that way. He didn't even know I felt that way and I would never tell him. If I did, he would come back home without a second thought. He would drop everything for me. I stared at Mum across the table. Her sweet smile sent a warmth through me and I realised how selfish I was. Liam was where he needed to be.

I had to try and keep living too.

Mum went to work. I cleaned my room a little, and the rest of the house. I snuggled on the sofa watching another classic black and white movie. Although I wasn't a spoiled heiress, I related to the main character. She was a girl running away from her family. A girl running towards what she knew she wanted. I wasn't running away from my family – I had been pushing mine away, bit by bit – for their protection. The film was sweet and simple. The lack of colour made me feel safe. That day I wasn't as invested in the story as I could've been. I just turned the TV on to help focus my thoughts on something else. I stared at the screen without really absorbing the plot. It was like I had no interest. My mind dazed. I didn't know what my real interests were anymore. Keeping myself in darkness was my only concern. My task.

My phone beeped.

It was a text from Kai. The corners of my mouth rose. A distraction.

Kai: Are we boyfriend girlfriend?

My slight smile vanished. My heart sank. I wasn't sure if I wanted a boyfriend. I wasn't sure if that was something I was ready for.

Me: I don't know.

Kai: Do u think you'd want to be my girlfriend?

Me: Is this u asking?

Kai: Well I would've done some sort of grand gesture that showed how much I care and writers would've stolen to put into movies, but this morning I woke up with this question stuck in my mind and now we're firmly into the afternoon and I still can't shake it away. I don't like not knowing this type of thing.

Me: So this is u asking then?

Kai: Yes.

I thought about his question. Swayed myself to an answer. No.

I convinced myself it was the right one and convinced myself again. I was getting ready to send him a text – even though I knew it was the answer he didn't want to hear and I quickly realised that would be the moment I would lose him. From then on I would no longer see his beautiful eyes. His colours. His light. I didn't want to think what would happen to my world. The colours Kai brought would no longer exist and I didn't think I would find the strength anytime soon to create my own and make them believable – liveable.

My phone beeped. The sound shook away the overflowing thoughts. Another text from Kai.

Kai: Hold on. Let's do a questionnaire. (But let me remind u I'm at work and might be fired if the bosses catch me using my phone so much – so it's your fault if we're broke.) So please tell me you'll accept this as my (not so) grand gesture.

Kai's words somehow slipped a lightness in me. My muscles felt relieved. Half of me was locked with a firm "No". But the other half was curious.

Me: A questionnaire?
Kai: Yeah. Will u accept it as my grand gesture?
Me: We'll see.

I didn't know why I played along. My mind knew what was best.

Kai: Throughout my shift I'll send questions ur way and all u have to do is answer Y or N. Ready?
Me: Y.
Kai: Good start!

A couple of seconds later my phone beeped. I read his message.

Kai: Do you like Kai Pearson? Y or N.

Me: Y.

I did like Kai. I related to him. Resonated with his story –
his past. He was smart and charming and a good person. *Why
wouldn't I like him?*

Kai: Do u think Kai Pearson is either cute, hot and/or
sexy?

Me: Y.

Kai: To which one??

Me: N.A.

Kai: U can't just do that!

Me: N.A.

Kai: OK. Do u like spending time with Kai Pearson?

Me: Y.

Kai: Are u comfortable around Kai Pearson?

Me: Y/N.

Half of me felt elated when in his presence. As if I could do
anything. As if I was capable – better than OK. But the other
half of me remained in my darkness. Unprepared to see the
light. Unprepared to accept it.

Kai: That question can be reviewed at a later date. Do u
feel like u can tell Kai Pearson your secrets?

Me: N/Y.

I shared my secrets through my art. Since I wasn't creating art anymore I wasn't sharing my secrets. But that didn't mean they didn't exist.

Kai: Understandable. Will u admit to having a crush and/ or feelings of like/love for Kai Pearson?

I laughed.

Me: Y.

His blunt honesty and bright confidence was what had made me like him in the first place. I wasn't one to run around town or stand on rooftops screaming my confessions of undying love – pre- or post-accident. But I did like Kai. I couldn't deny it. Not a single part of me tried to convince myself otherwise. Which made me nervous. Unprepared. Guarded.

Kai: Will you be my girlfriend?
Me: Y.
Kai: OXOX

I didn't know what had come over me. Earlier that day I was locked with a firm 'No'. But now, it seemed, I was willing to take the risk.

Chapter TWENTY-THREE

A burst of a need to draw stroked my veins. I hadn't felt that in a long time and I didn't want to ignore it. I was willing to take the chance and was home alone so nobody would see.

I found an unused art book and some pencils in my bedroom. Before the accident, if an idea popped into my mind at any time, I would draw it down so I wouldn't forget, then elaborate on it in my Art Cave. Assembling at the kitchen table I began to draw. The grey pencil moved across the smooth paper and I began to draw who I'd secretly been longing to. As I etched the lines creating the curve of the eyes, a weight decreased. I erased my mistaken lines and felt a release.

Slowly my hand reached for a watercolour pencil. It felt heavy, like the brightness was weighing down my fingers. I stared at it in my hand. It was like the colour glared at me. I squinted. I looked at my sketch. The pencilled features seemed too grey to represent what I wanted to capture. My eyes wandered to the colour in my hand. In that moment I wasn't ready to risk producing an image with such colours. I tossed the pencil back into the case and slid it from my reach, yet still felt its bright presence, almost as if it were burning my skin. I shut my eyes and fixed on darkness. My almost serenity.

Later, examining my sketch, I wasn't disappointed that colour was not yet included. I had created something. I had taken the risk. Maybe I could trust myself again with my art, and not subconsciously unveil my secret.

Mum and I convened at the dinner table. The wooden four-seater was in the centre of the small room, spaced far enough away from the windows and small table in one corner that held a fake fern in a striped plant pot. Although Mum loved flowers she wasn't blessed with green thumbs. The dining area was just two steps away from the shiny white kitchen. The cupboard doors looked like they were laminated. Mum loved it because they were so easy to keep clean. The dark worktop was home to our much-loved mixing machine, kettle and cookie jar. The dimly lit space felt warmer, since we'd left the door open to the lounge. The heat poured through, making the floorboards a little warmer to step on.

We ate a home-made quiche with salad. As the days passed my appetite slowly grew. I found I was hungrier when Mum was around. Maybe it was another form of evidence to convince her I was alive and well. *I think that's what I wanted.* We were faced with dessert. I knew we ate a light meal for a reason. We both stared at our own large piece of store-bought chocolate Mars cake. It was our favourite, and tonight she wanted to spoil us, just because.

Both halfway through our large slices, the richness began to slow us down.

"So P, how are things with Kai?"

"Good … He just asked me to be his girlfriend."

Mum smiled as she slowly lit up. "And what did you say?"

"I said Y."

"What?"

"Y, as in the letter."

She looked at me confused. My brain put two and two together and realised she thought I meant 'Why'. I released a breathy laugh. "We did this questionnaire thing and he asked me to answer Y or N. Yes or no."

"So you said yes?"

"Yes, I said yes."

"My little girl's got a *boyfriend*?"

"Mum!"

"What?"

"Don't act all weird."

"I'm not. Aw … P, that's lovely. How nice."

I saw a fleck of hope sketched across her face. I could almost read her mind. She was glad I was "getting back out there".

"Make sure he treats you right. We both know the consequences if he doesn't. Like him being paraded down the streets in just ladies underwear or none at all. And the potential removal of his *manhood*. Maybe we should invite him around for dinner one night and I'll talk to him about the conditions and penalties he might endure if he hurts my baby girl."

"Mum!" I laughed.

"Well do actually invite him around for dinner, P. It'd be nice to see him again."

"I'll see when he's free."

Chapter TWENTY-FOUR

A few days later, Kai came round for dinner. Mum made so much pasta you'd think we were feeding the entire street. I told her he liked to eat. He was a growing boy and liked his food. Maybe he'd told her about his plans to do a forty-hour famine that I didn't know about, so maybe she wanted to stuff him full to bursting. Either way, I could tell she was happy there was another mouth to feed.

The doorbell rang.

Before I answered it, I quickly re-briefed Mum on how to act a little more nonchalant. Although she's easy to talk to and understanding, for some reason when guests are around she likes to morph into this over-doting parent. I also told her not to share my embarrassing stories. Especially about the one with me face planting the mud that wasn't exactly mud, when we went horse riding a few years ago.

I opened the door. Winter was still strong. The cold air clutched around my legs. I made Kai quickly step inside so I could shut the door and remain in warmth.

"Hi."

Kai kissed my cheek then unwrapped his scarf. "Hello Peyton."

I bit my lip. My stomach fluttered. *Was I nervous?*

"Is everything OK?"

I took a deep breath and nodded my head. "Yeah. Yep. Good. All good."

I was nervous. I turned away from his kind stare and the oddly cute way he held onto his scarf, and made my way to the kitchen. He followed me. I could feel him.

"Hello Emma. Something smells amazing."

"Hey Kai. Lovely to see you again." Mum walked straight up to him and placed a kiss on his cheek. I half expected her to spill an embarrassing story about me, like the time I walked into glass doors (they didn't sense my presence so they didn't open). I don't think I could ever forget the sound of Mum's cackling – after she'd checked that I was OK. I knew she was always going to say what she wanted, but I thought I'd give it my best shot to limit her story times.

"Come and sit down. Dinner will be ready soon." She pulled out a chair at the dining table and Kai sat down.

His hair was tied in a bun. Pulled completely from his face, it highlighted his handsome features – including his beautiful eyes. I never usually liked guys with long hair, I thought they always looked better with shorter hair. But I liked it on him. He pulled it off without even trying. He took off his grey waist-length coat and placed it on the back of his chair. He wore a navy blue knitted jumper with a wide collar that had two large brown buttons near the neck, and his usual black jeans. I expected to see his much-loved boots, but that night he wore pointed dress shoes. Yet another entire look and style that he pulled off perfectly. He was beginning to make me feel like the casual jeans and jumpers and other baggy clothes I wore weren't enough.

Mum checked the saucepans filled with food, gave each one a quick stir then joined us at the table. "So, Kai, how've you been? Has it been busy at the coffee shop?"

"I've been good … Living life. Forcing myself to enjoy this winter." He looked at me and smiled.

Did he remember winter was my favourite season?

"Work's been good. Nothing too exciting … Although the other day this woman found a random coin from Canada in her bag and took it as a sign that her ex-lover wants her back. The lover's Canadian. She told me she was going to book a flight and leave in the next couple of days. She could be on her way right now. It's a shame we'll probably never know how that turns out."

I smiled. Using his imagination and elaborating on the simplest of things until he could do it no more, was the way Kai saw the world. He seemed to always see the best in people.

"Now that *is* a shame," Mum said. "We're just going to have to predict what happened in the end. Did she book a flight? Did she get on the plane?"

"Did her ex want to see her?" Kai said.

"Does the ex she told you about even exist?" I said.

"If they did meet, has her ex moved on already?" Mum said.

"Is the love they once shared strong enough for a second try?" Kai said.

"Oh, good one." Mum said.

I smirked at the two of them. They were both enjoying themselves. I leant back and listened. I was never that good at making up stories from the top of my head anyway.

"I think we should go with she booked the flight and met her lover. They were both filled with emotion because of their break-up and the sweet memories of their past relationship, *and* the fact she flew thousands of miles for the speck of a chance that they could be together again, that they started dating again," Kai said.

"Yeah … They took a chance. Things weren't perfect. They had their rough patches. But they stayed together." Mum smiled. "I like a happy end."

My heart struck with a little pain. I felt bad that my mum didn't have the happily ever after she wanted. The happily ever after she deserved.

"So Kai, what are your intentions with dating my daughter?"

Kai smiled. I knew he knew my mum asked through a jokey tone, but he answered honestly. "Certain aspects of our future relationship are unclear, as they should be I think. But my intentions are to treat her the best I can. I want her to fall in love with me, head over heels, and be so captivated and consumed by me and our love, that in her mind, nobody else is good enough apart from me. I intend to do this in the healthiest way possible."

Mum looked impressed and slightly shocked. But I couldn't read the other expression on her face. "And how are *you* going to feel about *her*?" Her tone was different now. Serious.

Kai answered like he had prepared for it his whole life. "As I think you already know, Emma, I'm intrigued by your daughter. Everything about her I want to know. I want to understand. I'm falling in love with her, but I don't think she knows that. Maybe she will now that I've said it out loud. I'm already captivated by what we share and how much I feel for her. And I'm waiting patiently for the love, she might in time, give me. I already know no one else will match, compare or reach her standards, or perfection if you will. Together I want us to just, be."

"Wow … He's a keeper." Mum removed herself from the table and checked on the food.

Kai and I remained seated. I didn't know what I should have said back to him. He was so brave about the way he felt about me and the way he wanted me to feel about him, the way he saw our relationship growing. I'd never even really thought about it. A part of me wanted to leap from my chair and kiss him passionately. Tell him I wanted all of that too. Tell him that being with him made me happy. Made me feel hope. Made me feel stronger. The other part of me wanted to run and hide, because now I was even more afraid that I wouldn't be enough.

The doorbell rang.

"Who's that? Are we expecting something?"

"Can you get that P, while I finish dishing dinner out?"

When I answered the door, I felt lighter.

"Liam!"

"What's going on, P?"

"What are you …" I couldn't believe he was there. "What are you doing *here?*"

Liam stepped inside and closed the door. I wrapped my arms around him. His clothes were cold. We squeezed each other tight. He lifted me off the floor. His arms locked around my core and I couldn't breathe, but I didn't care. As he placed me back on the ground, I felt my ear-to-ear smile.

"Mum and I planned a surprise dinner for you tomorrow night. Then she told me that your boyfriend was coming tonight. I couldn't pass up the opportunity to meet him, so I came down a night earlier. Where is the lucky lad?"

Liam was a confident person. A "party starter" Mum liked to call him. He marched straight up to Kai and stuck out his hand. "Hey. I'm Liam, Peyton's brother."

Kai stood and shook Liam's hand. "I'm Kai. She's told me a bit about you. It's nice to meet you."

"You too."

I saw Liam inspecting him. He made it obvious enough.

"So *you're* the coffee-shop kid?" Liam said.

"Is that the title I've been given?" Kai looked to Mum and me.

"In earlier conversations," Mum said. "But you're more than that now." She smiled warmly.

The four of us spent hours chatting. Kai seemed to fit in just right, as if there was a perfect space for him to squeeze into. He happily and quite easily followed our banter and wasn't shy to chime in with his own remarks. I was given the nod of approval from Liam when Kai wasn't looking, and I already knew Mum liked him.

Later that night, when Kai was going home, he left me with a kiss on my cheek then kissed my knuckles like he had at the end of our third date.

A sparkling force lingered around the house. I scanned the room and could see how it all connected. The glow from the moon thrust though the window, grazing the glass on the photo frames and sending a thin line of light to the lamps. The bulbs' brightness spread across the room like the early-morning sunrise, making Mum's earrings sparkle almost as much as her eyes. Her laughter glimmered to Liam. Seeing them smile warmed my insides. That moment was a light I wanted to soak in. Bask in.

I was glad Liam had come, and for once I was even happy that he and Mum had kept it a surprise. Having the three of us under one roof felt right. It reminded me of the many morning moments we used to share before we went our separate ways for the day.

Liam and I helped Mum with the dishes. After a little while we went to bed. I rested under my warm blankets. I smiled and breathed the deepest breath I'd breathed since returning home from hospital. I took a moment and relished the blissful light.

Chapter TWENTY-FIVE

My phone beeped loudly and startled me awake. My eyes searched for my alarm clock – it was six in the morning. I half-heartedly rummaged for my phone on the bedside table. Through half-opened eyes, I read the text.

Kai: Good morning! Thanks for dinner last night. Your family is exceptional!

Me: Morning. I'm glad u enjoyed yourself … Is everything OK?

Kai: Why wouldn't it be?

Me: We're messaging at 6 am.

Kai: Did I wake you?

I began typing my response.
My phone beeped.

Kai: Be honest.

I erased my unfinished text.

Me: Y.

Kai: Sorry.

Me: It's fine. Is there anything else on ur mind other than ur appreciation for last night's Swift family festivities?

Kai: Well I was wondering if you're free Friday night?

Me: For what?

Kai: Another date. I've got a good idea.

Kai: Scratch that. A great idea. Something fun I promise!

Me: What is it?

Kai: Can't say unless u agree to the date. OX

Me: Fine. I agree to the date. What is it?

Kai: Actually can u let me keep it a surprise until Friday? I'll tell u the plan before we leave.

Me: Why can't u tell me now?

Kai: I want to keep u in suspense.

Me: That's not necessary.

Kai: But it makes life fun.

Me: I guess I'll see u Friday then.

Kai: Can't wait! OXOX

Later that day Mum, Liam and I went out for dinner. My heart felt whole when the three of us were together. I felt home. I felt better than OK.

We arrived at the small restaurant for an early meal. The space was congested with tables but was fairly empty of patrons. Two elderly couples sat together for a double date and a large family with young children huddled around a long table for what looked like a birthday party. The ceiling lights beamed upon the shiny silver chairs place around rectangular tables. Cutlery already arranged and salt and pepper shakers sat in the centre of the tables, alongside napkin holders. We were shown to our table. A four-seater by the window. The view was of the dampened chewing-gum stained street and several cars parked down the road. A light in a shop across from us began to flicker. It made me wonder what Kai would think and the meaning he would find behind it. Maybe it was Morse code, a message to a secret society or a loved one.

"So Liam, how are the studies going? Are you still enjoying the course?" Mum said.

"It's all going great, Mum. Fine and dandy."

"Oh no. What's happened?"

"What?"

"Sweetheart, I've known you for your entire life and your definitions of fine and dandy are *not* what's written in the dictionary. Now tell me what's happened."

Liam looked at me. His bright eyes were bulging with worry and his relentless attempt to hold in his laughter. I stared back at him, our eyes conversing. Without a word he was pleading with me to have his back. Change the subject. Avert the attention. I knew Liam and I had been staring at each for too long when Mum started questioning me.

"Peyton? Do *you* know something?"

"Uh …"

"You see …" Liam began.

I stupidly butted in. "Liam told me about this party …" Regret splurged as the words left my mouth, realising he probably had this whole speech prepared. But I wanted to try and help him. I was never good at making stories up on the spot, but when Liam was there helping out, I always seemed to manage. "And these students played a crazy prank."

"At *your* school?"

"No Mum." Liam said. "It was at this other school."

"Yeah this other school, someplace else and it happened *years* ago." I waved my hands around. "He read about it online."

"OK. So why are you acting weird about a prank some kids did years ago at a different school?"

"I'm not acting weird."

Mum eyed him.

I could tell Liam was close to admitting the truth. I could see the words on the tip of his tongue.

"Well Mum …" He swallowed them away. "There was talk at my school that some members of the student body were considering remastering the prank. When I heard what was happening I told my friends I didn't want to be involved. I put my foot down, Mum. I said I wouldn't do it. I didn't want to. It was too dangerous. The consequences would've been too severe. Expulsion if we – *they* – got caught."

I scrambled through memories, stories and words, just to try and divert the attention from him. He could usually keep a secret but when Mum gave him that stern, knowing look, it was like he was eight years old again – when he confessed to eating the entire chocolate cake and smothering some chocolate on my face so I could take some of the fall. I was panicking and spoke about the first thing that came to mind. "I've been working on new art." My heart sank. I really didn't want this to be a topic I discussed with Mum and Liam. Up till now I would always tell them about my art or the new artist I was obsessed with that month. And I loved sharing it with them, because they were so supportive. Countless times the three of us had researched the closest art exhibition and spent the day there. Liam pretended to be the world's snobbiest and loudest art critic, and it got to a point where Mum and I would have to go to the exhibits in secret.

Their sights set on me, Mum suspiciously glanced at Liam, with a smirk on her face. I knew she knew he wasn't telling the whole truth. Secretly, I was happy he hadn't told her. Not that I liked it when we lied to her, more the fact that I knew he was able to keep something from her. It made me feel better about hiding my dark side from her. It made me feel all right to be keeping my secret from her too.

Friday arrived quicker than expected. As I got ready for our date, I thought back on my week. Nothing was different. I had spent my usual hour with Dr Wilson. He had tried to get me to dig a little deeper, to speak of the darkness I held. But I didn't. He had showed me another drawing he'd created, which I liked. I liked that he wanted to show me his art. That he was doing something that he liked and seemed genuinely happy to share it with me. As per request, he also showed me photographs of the graffiti-type artwork he had made for his friends' skateboards when he was younger. It was actually really good.

As the days passed I had still kept my thoughts at bay. Kept my memories in the shadows. During the last few nights I'd only woken up in a rush of sweat once. My nightmares seemed to be fading, allowing me to rest in peace. But it did make me wonder if they were gradually creeping to the forefront of my mind, ready to attack me – with no respite – during the light of day. Ready to hit me when I wasn't expecting it.

The doorbell rang. Liam answered it.

I was in the bathroom but heard every word they said.

"Hey Kai, come in. You all right?"

"Yeah, I'm good. How about you?"

"I'm great. You wanna come and sit down?"

I quietly opened the bathroom door. It squeaked a little. I tiptoed down the hall and leant my back against the wall, my ear close to the doorframe.

"You want a drink of anything?" Liam said.

"Ah, no. I'm fine thanks."

"So what are you and Peyton up to tonight?"

"It's a surprise."

"You're not going to tell me where you're taking my sister?"

"I ..."

"You're not off to a good start, kid."

Liam seemed a little harsher than usual. Maybe he was being overly protective because of my crash. I could just picture him staring squarely at Kai. That same look he uses when he asks a question once and waits until he gets the answer he wants.

"Well I was thinking of taking her to the arcade to play a couple of games and go bowling."

I kind of felt guilty for listening in on their conversation, but was relieved to know where Kai and I were off to. I had built-up tension caught within me. I know Kai and I had been alone together, but some days were easier than others. Hearing the simple word "arcade" made that worried feeling go away. I silently started preparing myself for the date. The people. The sounds. The colours.

"The arcade huh?"

"Yeah."

"Well don't let her play air hockey. She always cheats at that."

I did not. I played fair and square. Liam just hated losing to his little sister.

Kai chuckled. "Any other advice?"

My insides clenched. Liam had always been protective of me. Sometimes it made my stomach turn. Sometimes he made it so embarrassing – even if it was in a jokey tone – but it proved that he cared. That he loved me.

"Don't be an idiot. And look after her."

"I will. I mean, I *won't* be an idiot. I *will* look after her."

I snickered quietly. Kai was nervous.

"Good. 'Cause if you hurt her I won't think twice to … "

"Hi." I stepped into the lounge. Although I loved Liam's protectiveness, I didn't want Kai to feel disheartened, especially now that he was my boyfriend. And knowing the destination of our date, I thought we would have fun. "Sorry to keep you waiting."

"That's OK." Kai smiled but I saw the nervousness in his eyes.

"So what have you guys been talking about?"

"Football," Liam said.

"Oh. Kai I didn't know you enjoyed football."

"Yeah, I do … I mean, I'm not the biggest fan. My stepdad loves it though. We've been to a few games together. It's good fun. And I've been thinking recently to get into it more, you know …"

"Well Liam's a huge fan of every sport under the sun. Other than duck shooting. I'm sure he'd be able to teach you a few things."

"Yeah." Kai nodded.

I couldn't help but smile. "Are you ready to go then?"

"Yep."

I walked over to my brother and looked him in the eyes. "Bye Liam."

He smiled and gave me a cheeky wink before he sprang from the sofa and squeezed me tight. "See you later. Have fun."

"See you later, Liam." Kai raised his hand slightly in an attempted wave.

We made our way to the front door. I quickly slipped my shoes on.

"Be good, you two!"

Kai and I stepped outside. I forced a breath out which became fog. "So, you haven't told me where we're off to yet."

"Right. Yeah. Um, I thought that maybe we could go to the arcade. Are you up for bowling?"

"Sounds like fun."

The music from the large arcade games, bowling balls striking the pins and the laughter of customers filled my ears. The noise variations allowed me to focus on a number of things. Kept my mind busy. Distracted. I stood to the side as Kai made his way to the counter and bought a bunch of tokens. He strode back to me, his full colours reigniting.

"So what do you want to do first? Your choice."

I searched the low-lit room. Coloured lights from the arcade games layered across the space. My eyes found the air-hockey table. I smiled. "How about air hockey?"

"OK."

We stood at either end of the large table that had the scoreboard raised in the middle. The air from the sides rose up and brushed my face. With smirks on our faces we each held a mallet. I felt the competitiveness bubble. Kai dropped the puck on the table. He hit it towards me and it bounced from the barrier back to his side of the table. When the puck came back to me, I knocked it with one fell swoop, lunging into the slot. I looked up at the scoreboard – one nil.

Kai took the puck from his end then shook his wrists. He bounced up and down and performed a couple of simple stretches. I lightly bit my lip to stop myself from laughing. He cracked his neck, rolled his shoulders, then aligned his mallet and the puck. His eyes targeted the goal. He hit the puck with such force it bounced in and out of my goal and straight into his.

"No!" He clutched his hair.

This time I couldn't stop myself from laughing.

Kai pointed to the scoreboard. "I let you have that one … *two* actually. But I can't be so giving anymore. The air hockey gods gave me this gift and it would be a shame to hide it away."

We played three games. Each one I won, proving that my talent at air hockey wasn't a hoax.

"You know, when I was talking with Liam before we left, he told me you cheat at air hockey."

"Did he now?"

"And after being defeated a few times, I might have to agree with him."

"What? I won fair and square."

"Well I wouldn't say fair …"

"But the air-hockey gods gave you *the gift*, doesn't that make *you* the cheat?"

"They clearly gave me the gift of *losing*. Who knew I was playing against such a pro?"

Next we played hoop shooting. Kai grabbed the basketballs and flicked his wrist with ease, only missing one basket and getting the highest score and a bunch of tickets.

"Why do I get the feeling basketball is more your sport than football?"

"Well it kind of is. But I do like football. Really."

"I believe you. Can I have a go?" I played a round and I wished I hadn't asked for a turn. I was useless at sport. I had never really been an overly competitive person and took a shine to inside activities.

"Do you want another turn?" Kai said.

"I don't know. That round was pretty awful,"

"Come on, you can do it." He smiled.

"OK, but if this round turns out to be worse than my first try, you have to promise me you'll erase the memory from your mind."

"Promise."

Kai placed the tokens in the machine. The large red numbers counted down.

5, 4, 3, 2, 1.

A buzzer sounded. The basketballs were released. The timer was set. In a rush I reached for a ball and threw it into the hoop. I continued throwing them, trying to keep up a momentum. Kai had made it look so easy. As the time fell away, Kai reached for the balls too. He didn't miss a shot.

The buzzer sounded again. Time was up.

"Hey, look at that!" I smiled as I high-fived Kai. "Fifth on the leader board!"

"Now I don't have to erase that memory of you."

I smiled at the floor as I tucked my hair behind my ear.

"So are you up for bowling now? Or did you want to grab something to eat?"

Kai and I exchanged our shoes for bowling shoes then made our way to our designated aisle. We each picked a couple of bowling balls and placed them on the ball-return machine.

"Ladies first."

I clutched the heavy ball with my three fingers, resting it in my other hand as I lifted it to my chin and walked to the line. Music played through the speakers. I didn't know what the song was called, or who it was by, but I liked the beat. Pins from the other aisles crashed to the wall. Voices cheered. Talking spread through the air. I liked the sounds. The distractions. I focused on the ten pins in front of me. Adjusted my stance. Pulled my arm back. Brought it forward then released the ball. I knocked down a few pins. Then went for my second ball.

We were just over halfway through our second game and I had somehow thrown two strikes.

It was my turn again.

Kai began to commentate. "Peyton grabs the ball. Adjusts her hold until it's right."

I smiled at him.

"Miss Swift is fairly new to the Annual Pearson Bowling Tournament, but it looks like this isn't her first rodeo."

I stood listening to his comments and chuckled, unable to take my next shot seriously.

"She's about to strut her way to the line. Ladies and gentlemen, your eyes do not deceive you – if she gets this strike, she will have made a turkey."

I stepped away.

"She's going for it!"

I looked back and laughed. It felt good to. I shook my head, focusing my thoughts, and followed through on my shot. The pins crashed to the wall and spread across the shiny floor. I threw my fist in the air.

"She's gone and done a turkey!"

Kai and I bounced towards one another. Our hands clapped in a double high-five. He took his hands and gently touched my cheeks as he brought his face down to mine and kissed my lips. His arms wrapped around me, lifted me off the ground then spun me round. He set me down. A large smile printed across his face as he walked towards the ball-return machine and gripped his bowling ball.

"My turn then, and no laughing if I don't get a strike. Have I even made one this game?"

I looked at the screen but my eyes didn't register what was written. "No." Without looking I found a seat, my bum only just setting on the edge. I almost fell to the floor and I hoped no one saw as I awkwardly adjusted myself. I felt my heart beating – it thrashed the blood through my veins. I wasn't numb. The sensation was still accessible. It was just my mind focused solely on the moment just passed.

Without blinking, I watched Kai bowl. We'd just shared our first kiss. I thought I liked it. It was quick. But it was sweet. Almost perfect for the moment. Or maybe it was just simply perfect. For some reason I hadn't thought we would be kissing that night. I'd *thought* about kissing him when we were on earlier dates, but that all seemed different now that we were boyfriend and girlfriend. I was captured in the spontaneity, my lips still tingling. I didn't focus on the dark, instead I latched onto the colours we made.

Kai picked up his second ball then walked back for his next throw. I found myself smiling. Happy our first kiss had happened like that. Knowing if it were more planned out, I would have talked myself out of it. I wouldn't have let it happen.

We finished bowling and received our own shoes. I liked the way he wasn't making our first kiss a big deal. It was unexpected. Fun. But I wanted to know what he was thinking. If he liked it. If it was OK.

We made our way to the cafeteria and ordered.

"So have you had fun?" Kai said, dunking his hot chips in sauce.

"Yeah."

"Well I got you to laugh a little. So that's progress."

"Hey, I laugh."

Kai smiled as he nodded.

"I *do*."

"I'm looking forward to hearing it more."

A stone turned in my stomach, weighing me down. I

suddenly felt a pressure to always be this fun girl. This girl who goes along with things. Who absorbs her surroundings. The colours. The sounds. The girl who laughs, who's happy. But I wasn't always that girl. When I was with him, that girl got to shine through – when I let her – but most of the time I was afraid to set her free. To allow myself to let go. I'd allowed the darkness – my past – to leach its way into my every day. It was hard to detach from how it had intertwined itself into my thoughts and the moments that were supposed to keep me happy.

Instead of replying I took a sip of my drink. Twirled the melting ice cubes with the straw. I didn't know what I should have said.

Before we made our way outside Kai told me to wait by the door. A few minutes later he came walking towards me.

"Close your eyes and hold your hands out." Kai said.

"What?"

"I got you something."

"What?"

"Close your eyes."

I held out my open palms and quickly shut my eyes, wanting to open them as soon as possible. I felt something small drop into my hands.

"You can open them now."

I looked to see a small basketball keychain. My smile grew.

"With the tickets we won, it was either that or a miniature slinky that was extremely stubborn. We can grab the slinky if you prefer."

"No. It's perfect."

"Do you know you have to win something like a *billion* tickets, well not exactly a billion, but a *lot* of tickets to get something from the top shelf?"

We made our way to the car. As soon as we stepped outside the smell of rain sprang into my nostrils. The pavement was soaked. Small puddles scattered on the ground. It wasn't raining anymore, but the clouds remained grey. As the sky continued darkening into night, the stars began to sparkle.

Kai kept his promise to my mum to be a gentleman as he opened the passenger door. I got inside and buckled up, still silently questioning what he was thinking. We drove to my house.

"Knock knock," Kai said.

"Really?"

"Come on … knock knock."

"Who's there?"

"Ya."

"Ya who?"

"Wow. You sure are excited to see me."

I laughed. The jokes he told were really lame but that's what made them better. Laughter gave me a feeling like I was releasing clumped-up energy. I liked laughing. I wanted to do it more. Maybe Kai would get to see my smile more.

He told me a story about when he and his two little brothers were caught playing a practical joke on their dad, by hiding his car keys and all of his shoes. Their mum got them to clean the lounge until she could see it shine, and the fact that his brothers were quite a bit younger than him, resulted in him doing most of the work.

Kai walked me to the doorstep. I was happy to let the colour in. Kai was the only bright place I felt safe in. When I was around him it felt OK to catch a glimpse of colour. To acknowledge it. To not be afraid.

"Thanks for tonight," Kai said. "It was fun. And next time I will beat you at air hockey."

"We'll see about that."

Kai kissed my cheek then locked his arms around me. His hugs were strong and warm. I couldn't help but feel secure within them. He slowly moved back, keeping his head close to mine. I could hear him deciding whether to kiss me. I could hear him pondering whether I was OK with it or not. I lifted my face slightly closer to his. He closed his eyes and I kissed him. My body tingled. Our lips sparked.

"Sweet dreams, Peyton Swift."

Kai made his way to his car.

I stepped inside and smiled. I didn't even try to erase it. Or dispose of the light I was exuding. And for the first time in what felt like forever, I believed that I was going to be OK. Better than OK.

Chapter TWENTY-SIX

The next morning I woke with a smile on my face. I wanted to keep it there for as long as I could. Until it no longer felt natural. Until it no longer sent a surge of happiness through me. I shoved my hair into a messy bun and wrapped myself in my dressing gown then made my way down the hall. A sweet aroma drifted towards me. I stepped into the kitchen to find Mum baking and Liam stationed at the worktop.

"What's all this?"

"Mum's making pancakes," Liam said.

"Yum." I plonked myself on the stool next to Liam. "Is there anything I can do to help?"

Mum pointed to a collection of jars and small bowls. "You guys can just grab those toppings and take them to the table."

Liam and I grabbed the toppings and placed them in the middle of the table. Mum had already set it with knives, forks and plates. We sat down to a large plate heaped with golden pancakes.

"Breakfast is served, my lovelies."

The three of us stacked pancakes on our plates and topped them with ice-cream, chocolate sauce and strawberries.

"So how was your date last night, P?" Mum said.

"Yeah Peyton, how was it?"

I laughed. "Stop it."

"What?" Liam said.

"Teasing."

"I'm not teasing. Just wondering how my baby sister's date went. Was he good to you?"

"Did you two have fun?" Mum said.

"Yes and yes." My smile grew. "We played a few arcade games and a couple of rounds of bowling."

"Did you beat him at air hockey?" Mum said.

"Three times."

"That's my girl."

The three of us kept talking as we filled our mouths with home-made pancakes. This moment was coloured to perfection.

"Liam, I dare you to eat your last pancake with a bunch of awful toppings that should *not* be put together."

"OK. What do I get out of it if I do?"

"Um ..."

"I want a drawing or a painting."

"Um ... OK. Deal."

Mum and I watched with disgust as Liam topped his pancake with mint-flavoured ice-cream, spray cheese, chocolate sauce and maple syrup, sprinkled with crushed cornflakes and olives.

"P, you dared me, remember. You can't judge." Liam scooped up his first forkful and chewed. "It's actually not that bad."

As we cleared the dishes, I smiled at the three of us. This moment reminded me of the time Mum got offered the full-time position at the hospital and Liam and I decided to make a feast for the three of us. I remember us searching for the best lasagne recipe online. When we finally chose one and got all the ingredients, we tried to follow the recipe as much as we could. We dropped ingredients all over the counter, which was covered in too many utensils. When it was finally in the oven, Liam went to his room and played on his PlayStation and I went to my Art Cave. I had my headphones in and I remember the foul stench. I rushed down the smoky hallway as Liam yelled out my name. He stood in the smoke clouds and chucked the burnt lasagne in the sink, whooshing his oven-mitt-covered hands around. I opened all the doors and windows and we both panicked, realising Mum would be home in twenty minutes. Luckily Liam had a good plan that required a little distraction on my part.

Mum arrived home and I told her to have a shower 'cause Liam and I had something special planned. When she came out of her room she asked where Liam was, as she made her way to the kitchen, but I grabbed her arm and directed her towards my Art Cave. All this while Liam rushed to the restaurant his friend worked at. Before he left he rang and explained the emergency. What felt like an hour later, Liam came and found us in my Art Cave. After my lame excuses to keep Mum in there, I think from then on she knew the best way to capture tone in a painting through the use of implementing shapes and colours in way more detail than she ever desired. The three of us made our way to the table that was set with three freshly baked pieces of garnished lasagne.

It was one of the best lasagnes we'd ever eaten. As the three of us stood at the sink washing and drying the dishes, Mum blurted out laughing and told Liam to thank his friend for making it. She said she knew we couldn't make something so delicious and that she smelt the burnt food halfway down the street. We all threw our heads back laughing.

I also thought of the countless fast-paced breakfasts we'd had before we went off to school and work. We'd rush through bites of food as we shoved books in our bags, then brush our teeth and button our clothes to look as presentable as possible in between the many times Liam and I fought over petty things – even though we'd both get over it in minutes.

Right now, I soaked up this moment, knowing how rare they were. Wanting to remember the details, I safely stored it away, making sure my darkness was unable to taint it.

I got washed and dressed then checked my phone to see one unread message. My heart flickered at the sight of his name.

Kai: Good morning. I hope u slept well. I have a question. But I don't know if I want to ask u just yet. I'm still deciding.

Me: You must ask me now. I'm intrigued.

I imagined him smiling at my use of the word "intrigued" because that was what he wanted me to be. And I was.

I flopped on my bed with a sketchbook and pencil and began to draw. I was so intrigued with eyes and smiles and faces that I would draw them without thinking. I also loved capturing the beauty of plants and animals and would incorporate them into my work. But people have always inspired me. Not knowing their stories fascinates me. I wanted to seek out their truth and express it through splattering and blending, gradually transitioning the colours as if it were their story growing. I would lift my paper or canvas and let the water paint run down the page. I loved how the effect could impact the tone and the meaning of my work.

I placed the pencil on the paper and began to shape a female's face without using a reference – just the fact that I had done it countless times before made me confident. A feeling I had been lacking.

Drawing came so naturally that before my mind truly registered what was happening, I was already comfortable with my action. There was no need to cease the flicking of the pencil in my fingers or pressing it down to allow for a darker line. The swift movement of my paper to angle it just so, allowing me to create the right shape, making me feel free. Creative. Happy. There was no need to force myself into my darkness.

My phone beeped.

I released my pencil but straight away I wanted to pick it back up.

I already knew the text was from Kai. I unlocked my phone and read his words.

Kai: OK then. How do u feel about my motorbike?

I took a deep breath and reread his question. We'd never spoken of his motorbike since the small mention at the start of our second date. My stomach turned.

Me: Fine.

Kai: How do u feel about going for a ride on my motorbike?

Me: Not so fine … I don't know??

Kai: Well take ur time to decide. I have an idea/plan for us.

Me: Will this idea/plan change if we don't go on the motorbike?

Kai: Y/N.

Kai: If u say Y to said motorbike ride, my idea/plan will kind of be symbolic.

Kai: No pressure though. You CAN say N.

Kai: OXOX

Still undecided, I stepped out of my room. I saw Liam tiptoeing down the hall. I was going to call out to ask what he was doing but I decided to follow him instead. I poked my head around the corner and my heart stopped. The door squeaked. "Liam!"

He pulled the half of his body that was stepping into my Art Cave back into the hallway.

"*What* are you *doing*?" My voice was loud. Stern.

He raised his arms in surrender. "Whoa, P."

I stomped to him and shoved his shoulders. His back hit the wall much harder than I anticipated.

"Ouch!" He clutched his shoulder. "P! What the *hell*?"

"*Don't* go in there! That's *my* Art Cave. That's *my* space."

"OK! Geez. No need to shove!"

I bit my tongue, hoping to stop the tears I could feel expanding.

"What? Have you got a dead body in there or something?"

I didn't reply. I folded my arms against my chest and stared at him with my jaw clenched. I stood my ground, hoping my lack of words would force him away.

Liam shook his head and left.

I walked past the lounge. He stared at the TV and didn't say anything. I went to the kitchen and got a drink then plonked on the sofa. I felt like I had to keep him in sight. I needed to know where he was. I couldn't have him see what was in my Art Cave.

I didn't know what he was watching, but these men were blowing something up. I kept my eyes forward then reached my palm out to him. I heard him snicker.

"Thanks." He said as he took the home-made cupcake.

I looked at him and softly grinned. Food was our go-to strategy when a peace offering was needed.

"I might need more than a cupcake this time, P. Like an explanation. What's going on with you?"

I kept my sight on the screen. The two men blew something up again. This time, the explosion was bigger. The damage was greater.

"Nothing." My panic flourished. I didn't know how well I could talk myself out of this one.

Later that day, I crouched at the front door and put on my shoes. As I was layered in clothes, my movements were somewhat restricted.

"Where are you off to?" Liam said.

I had to get out of the house. There was something I wanted to do, but the need to breathe was on top of my list. I wanted fresh air. I needed it.

It had been a couple of hours since my squabble with Liam, and he hadn't brought it up since I had pretended to be extremely invested in whatever TV show he had on. Truthfully, I couldn't recall anything that had happened on the screen. I was silently listing off excuses, making up stories, anything I could think of that would convince him to drop the subject. Something that would make him forget what had happened. So I decided to leave him home alone – to prove I trusted him. I had simply overreacted. And if he did go into my Art Cave, I would figure out an explanation to divert him from the truth.

"I'm going to see Kai at work. He messaged earlier, telling me he had an idea and wants me to think about my answer. I thought I'd try and coax out some more information from him in person."

"Want some company?"

"You can come if you want." I didn't mean to be as harsh as I was being. The words just fell out that way.

"Well will I be in the way?"

"You won't be in the way. If you want to come, come."

I waited for him to grab his jacket and beanie.

We slowly made our way to the coffee shop. The outside world was still grey. I watched as the dark, leafless tree branches swayed with the wind, like strokes from paintbrushes. The pavement was damp from the afternoon's rush of rain. A fresh breeze wrapped around my body, engulfing me within my colourless surroundings. I was glad it was winter. The world helped me stay inside my grey ways.

I still didn't want to see the light.

"So, has the coffee shop changed that much since the last time we were in it?" Liam said.

"No, not really. Obviously they've got different paintings."

"That's cool. Any of them you like?"

"Yeah, they're really good. I'm pretty sure it's work by two different artists. One of the collections is bright. Lots of colour. Filled with textures. The other is a little darker, like they've gone for a misty-fog theme. But they have a lot of detail. I think you'll like them."

"So are you going to tell me why you attacked me like a crazy person?"

"I'm sorry about that." I looked at him. "I *am*. I didn't mean to hurt you."

He nodded slowly.

"It's just you know I don't like anyone going in there and …"

"P, I've been in there *heaps* of times. Yes, most of the time I was in there when you were there, but what's the difference? It's not like I was going to steal something or ruin one of your pictures. You know I'd never do that."

"I know, it's …"

"It's what?"

Liam I've made paintings about my secret and I don't want you to see them. I don't want to see them. I don't want you to know.

"I haven't been in there since my crash."

"But the other night you said you've been drawing."

"I've been drawing in an art book I found in my room."

"Oh … But why haven't you been in?"

"For some reason it feels a bit overwhelming, and I don't know what to make … Hold on a second, why were *you* going in?"

"Well you owed me a drawing, remember? The taste of that pancake keeps coming back to haunt me. I've brushed my teeth four times! Plus, I've been thinking about getting a new tattoo and was hoping to find something."

"And now the real reason."

"OK, first off, *all* of that *is* true. You do owe me a drawing and I have been thinking about getting another tattoo and would love it to be designed by you–"

"And second?"

"I know at dinner you said you'd been drawing, but I thought that maybe because you haven't really been in an exceptionally creative mood lately, that if I showed you some of your old work you might be inspired. I'm sorry for intruding."

We walked in silence for a minute.

"Hey, I haven't had a chance to say thanks for having my back at dinner. It was a close one. I almost crumbled." Liam said.

"What are sisters for?"

"So how are things with Kai? Is he treating you right?"

"*Liam.*"

"I've got to make sure you're happy, P. I've got to know that he's a good guy. That's my job."

"He's treating me right. He's a good guy."

"You really like this kid then?"

I grinned. "Yeah." This was the first time I had really admitted how I felt about Kai to someone else. It felt nice to say the words. Part of me even felt relieved.

"Well, good." Liam nudged me.

After I regained my balance, we continued our slow stroll. I glanced at him. He was biting his lip. I knew what it meant when he did that. He had something he wanted to say. Something important.

"What is it?"

Liam looked at me, surprised. His blue eyes wide. "What?"

"What are you thinking? And *don't* tell me you're not. I know you are."

"OK. But, don't get angry, P, or try and push me away."

I stopped moving. Planted my feet on the path. Liam continued one more step until he realised then stepped back to me and looked me in the eyes.

"What is it?"

I saw him swallow the lump in his throat.

"I just wanted to ask you about how you're feeling, with the crash and things."

"I'm fine."

"P, I don't want to make you upset."

"I'm not. I already told you *and* Mum, I'm fine."

"OK. But, you can tell me though, if you're not. I'm good at keeping secrets, too."

I nodded, hoping my silent agreement would be the end of this conversation.

But it wasn't.

"It's just …" Liam stopped himself.

"Just say it, Liam." I needed to know what he was thinking. If there was something I could do to convince him to think of me differently. To see me differently. If there was something I could do to show him I was OK. That I was fine. Even if it wasn't the full truth.

"Before the accident, you seemed distant. I know it kind of sounds stupid 'cause I'm away at college and we don't see each other every day. But, I'd got used to our chats through technology. You'd send me random messages or videos of you painting in your Art Cave. And you kind of stopped doing that for a while. I was going to talk to you about it. Ask if things were OK, if I'd done something wrong. Then you were in the crash and, well, my world stopped."

Tears brimmed in my eyes. I didn't blink, in the hope that they would remain still. I separated my lips, wanting words to leave them. But before a sound escaped, Liam spoke.

"I've got to know that you're all right here, P. That you and Mum and are both happy, because I'll come back home without hesitating if you need me. Remember, before I left for college, you *promised* me you'd let me know if you or Mum needed me. You promised."

In that moment I wanted to beg him to stay. To admit I needed him. That without him there, I was empty. Without him there, I could never be fully happy. Part of me wanted to tell him about the darkness I craved and about the secret from my past that I had run from. Because I knew he could protect me.

But I couldn't. I couldn't ask him to drop his life for me. It wouldn't be fair.

I didn't know how I was pulling it off, but the tears in my eyes remained there. Not a single one rolled to my chin. I knew they wouldn't stay still for much longer. I stepped to Liam, stood on my tiptoes and latched my arms around his neck. I stared at the grey distance as my chin rested on his shoulder. I let my tears fall without sound as I breathed slowly. Liam wrapped his arms around me and stroked my back.

"I know the reward I want for my silence about your almost expulsion."

"Oh yeah, what is it?"

I squeezed him. "I want you to stay … I want you to stay at college, and promise me that you'll graduate. I want to see you in that cap and gown. I want to be that proud little sister cheering her big brother on from the audience."

"Deal." Liam kissed the top of my head. "But I better be able to hear you over the crowd."

"Deal." I wiped my eyes before we detached from our hug, realising I hadn't really answered his question. I hadn't given him any proof that I was OK. "Liam, I am OK. Speaking with Dr Wilson is really helping." I saw a speck of hurt gloss over his eyes and assumed it came from my confiding in a therapist and not him. I knew he'd never say that though; after all, he did help Mum talk me into going. And I knew he knew the sessions were helping me.

"That's good, P. I'm glad you're still going to therapy and that it's helping you."

I smiled the best I could. Hoped that I was beginning to convince him.

"Maybe I should head back home," Liam said. "I think I've already ruined your walk enough. I don't want to ruin your chat with Kai."

"No, don't go home. You've not ruined anything."

Liam flung his arm around my shoulder and we continued our walk.

We entered the coffee shop. It felt good to be out of the cold. I watched as Liam examined the art. It was the same canvases as the day Kai and I had met. The dream of having a piece of my own art in there sparked in my mind.

"Why don't you look around then grab us a seat while I order us something and quickly chat with Kai. It won't take too long."

"Take your time. No rush."

I ordered mine and Liam's drinks then made my way over to Kai. He smiled. I felt lighter inside but my thoughts were locked in the dark. I liked the way Kai looked at me. The way he made me feel like I was OK with him. Maybe more than OK.

"Hello Peyton. What you up to?" Kai continued to sweep the floor behind the counter while he spoke.

"Liam and I are just hanging out. Also, I came here to ask you if you could go into any more detail about said plan slash idea?"

"No can do. That would ruin the surprise. And before you say you don't like surprises, I think you'll like this one. I promise no school or mention of sensitive topics. Now that you know me, and I'm your boyfriend, I think that increases the trust between us … Do you trust me?"

Did I?

Could I?

Maybe.

"Yeah, but I …"

"If you're worried about the motorbike, you don't have to be. I'll take it slow, just like we did with our first car ride. I can't take it too slow, otherwise we'll fall off. But I'll keep you safe, just like I promised your mum."

I stared at him as I decided on my answer.

"Are you up for it then?" Kai asked.

His charming aura was weakening me.

"Yes. I'm up for it. But is there any chance this plan is happening anytime soon? I think I'd prefer it that way before I have the chance to change my mind."

"Is tomorrow soon enough?"

"Yeah. Until then I'll just not think about it." I turned around ready to make my way back to Liam and let Kai get back to his work, until I remembered something and turned back to him. "One more thing. Can we maybe not tell my mum about your motorbike or our motorbike ride? She'd freak and most likely chase you out of the house holding a frying pan high in the air if she found out."

"She's not a fan of them either?"

"Well I'm more of a fan than she is, but with everything that's happened, it's just easier if we keep it to ourselves."

"My lips are sealed. Another secret we keep … I like it."

I was about to step away.

"Wait!" Kai said. "Where do you want me to pick you up from?"

"Um … Here. Just tell me the time and we'll meet here tomorrow and go forth and conquer your said plan."

Chapter TWENTY-SEVEN

I told Mum I was going on a date with Kai and I didn't know when I'd be home. She wished us both a good time and told me to call her if I needed anything. The weather wasn't too cold as I made my way to the coffee shop. The air was calm and a soft breeze occasionally swept through, but it hadn't rained.

Nerves pricked at my insides. A mix of genuine nerves about my first time on a motorbike, intertwined with my excitement to spend time with my boyfriend. *My boyfriend. How weird.*

I saw Kai. He looked hot leaning against his jet-black bike, waiting for me. The motorbike seemed bigger – meaner – compared to the last time I had seen it. I felt my muscles soak up fresh nerves as if they were a sponge.

"Are you ready for this, Peyton Swift?"

"I don't think you can get more ready than I am right now,"

"Really?"

"No! I'm kind of scared and a little nervous. I don't know … I'm just trying to psych myself up."

Kai laughed at me. This simple sound made me ease up, if only a little.

A thin-toothed headband pulled his hair back and made it looked lighter. He rubbed his hands together as a smile grew. He bobbed up and down only just moving his knees. His brightness was bursting. I silently tried to boost myself up to a high-excited level, even though I knew I'd never reach his. Before he handed me his spare helmet, I plaited my hair and let it fall down my back, then placed the helmet on my head. Kai double-checked to make sure it was strapped tight enough.

Kai introduced me to his bike.

"Take a seat and I'll show you what everything does."

I cocked my leg over and sat down. As I planted my feet on the pavement, I gently placed my palms on the handlebars. The bike felt heavy. Foreign. Unpredictable. I released my grasp and lent back slightly. My eyes trailed over the left handlebar, home to the light switch and indicators.

"Just remember you've got to push the button in to turn it off. It doesn't automatically turn off like a car." Kai said that like I would be the one in control. "And directly below the indicators, you've got the horn."

My eyes followed his direction as he started to explain the right side.

"So right here, you have the kill switch, which is only used for emergency purposes but you leave it on all the time. And then you've got your throttle. Also, near where you rest your feet you've got your braking system. So the handlebar brake here on the right is just for the front wheel of the bike and the rear brake is near your feet. The handlebar brake is used most of the time, though."

I turned to follow Kai as he stepped back to my left side.

"So here you've got the clutch lever. You can give that a bit of a squeeze if you want."

I raised my hand to clasp the silver bar. It didn't do anything because the bike wasn't turned on. But my unsureness of this moment was starting to escalate.

The motion paused when Kai continued his explanation.

"And near your feet you have the gear shifter." He started telling me about the number of gears and what they each did, but stopped when he noticed the terms went over my head. "Sorry, you don't really need to know that. So that's basically it."

I stayed quiet.

"How do you feel?"

"All right … I guess." I remained on the bike. Even though my cautiousness was re-sparking, I wanted to go for the ride and wasn't going to let the voice inside my head talk me out of it. I wanted to feel something different. I wanted the adrenaline rush.

Slowly, I retouched the handlebars. They felt strong. Forceful. My fingertips lightly grazed the breaks. My hand travelled down to the smooth seat. My thoughts got lost in a familiar notion – the notion I had felt when I'd got in the car that night unsupervised. The notion I had felt just before my crash. Not caring what happened to me. Knowing that it was a risk I was taking. Putting myself on the line. Putting my body on the line and not caring if it broke, because I already felt broken.

I was ready. I wanted to ride.

I told Kai I was fine. I hopped off the bike. He cocked his leg over and found his stance. I scurried back on. I was ready for the rush. Kai told me to hold on really tight. He revved the engine. It was loud. A thunderous retort. I liked the sensation. He asked me if I was OK. I told him to start the ride before I could change my mind. I didn't want to lose the feeling I had uncovered.

We rolled to the road then whisked away. Blood rushed through my veins. My skin tingled. It was as if I could feel the adrenaline cooking inside me. I wanted more. I needed more. I wanted to hold onto the moment for as long as I could. As we swayed through traffic and journeyed along the road, I felt unrestricted. Somehow, I felt in control. As if I was driving my feelings. From the thrill of the ride I felt like I could run away from my darkness. My secret. My past.

I was almost ready to scream for Kai to go faster – drive until we were out of this town. This place. This world. I didn't know why I'd been so nervous. The ride made me feel alive. *I was alive. That was what I wanted.*

Kai didn't speed or break any road rules. He kept to his word. As we continued, I realised that was the closest we'd actually been to one another. Sure we had hugged before and we'd kissed, but our bodies hadn't been that close for long. I felt unsure, but I had no choice but to hold onto him. I squeezed him tight. I was scared to death but I wanted to be close to him.

My heartbeat hit his back and I wondered if he felt it too. He said he'd been working on a six-pack. I thought he'd said that to try and impress me – but I believed him now. His torso was lean. I closed my eyes and enjoyed having him close, then quickly opened them because I didn't want to miss this fast, new way to look at the houses that appeared smudged as we passed them. The trees and bushes that morphed together blending into a deep-brown, dirty-green wall. The roads were fairly empty but the cars we passed weren't by us for long. We whisked past them like we had superpowers. I wondered if that was the way Kai always saw the world.

The further we drove the fewer houses we passed. The only things I saw were blurry cows and wire fences that interweaved with grass that spread for ever. The crackling sound of the bike's engine echoed down the empty gravel road we now travelled down.

We arrived at our destination. Kai switched off the engine and parked the bike. I didn't want to come down from that high, but hopped off the bike and slipped out of my helmet to search our surroundings. Tall bare trees greeted us. The smell of damp bark and mud locked in my nose. "So what are we doing here?"

"Well Miss Swift, this is where we could've gone on our

first date, if you hadn't been too chicken to get on the bike. I will be honest and say I did hold slight judgement on you for not taking that risk, but now I understand why. So then, do you want to explore this forest?"

I smiled at him. "Yeah. I do … Now that we're here, I'm even more intrigued."

We made our way through the forest to Kai's secret place. I knew other people went there too because food wrappers were scattered on the ground. I hadn't been to this area in years. There are several different trails that are used more often during summer. Mum, Liam and I had walked most of them when I was younger. But exploring the outdoors was not my favourite activity.

On a dark winters day, I imagined that place being scary. The shapes of the trees and rustling sound of animals in near bushes would have caused me to question mine and Kai's safety. But that day, the weather was lighter. Cold. But a lighter grey. The sun tousled behind thin clouds, trying to shine. The rays intertwined through the branches, creating shadows on the forest ground.

Kai had brought food and a picnic blanket and we made ourselves comfortable, like that place was our home. I kept my bag near my side. I felt like the contents were screaming at me, commanding me to reveal what was inside. If I didn't take it out now it would burn a hole and make its own way to Kai.

"I brought you something."

"I told you, you didn't have to bring anything," Kai said. "I thought we agreed I'd bring everything."

"No, not food."

"Oh, OK."

I turned to my bag and took a deep breath. I shuffled through the contents and found what I was looking for then held on to it as I debated, eventually pulling out an A4 piece of paper. I turned around to face him.

"What's this?"

"I've drawn something. I want to show you."

Kai crossed his legs and sat up straight like he was a little boy about to open a birthday present. I handed the paper to him. He gazed at it, inspecting every part of it. Every line I had painted. Every mark on the page.

My first creation post-accident was a portrait of Kai. I had used watercolours – my favourite medium. I had made his blue/brown eyes the main focus under the colour markings splattered across the paper. It was the way I thought he saw the world. All colours. Every shade.

After what felt like half an hour, he smiled his cheeky smile. "Thank you."

Thank you? That was not really the response I was looking for. Was that a thank you for drawing him? Or a thank you for showing him my work?

"What do you think? Do you like it?"

I needed to know.

"Peyton it's incredible. You should do art more often." He chuckled at his own joke. "Why'd you draw me?"

I didn't really want him to ask that. Actually, I hadn't expected him to ask that. And now he had, I had to explain. Trying to find the right words, I said; "I drew you because you're unlike anyone I've ever known. The way you see the world, the colours you see it in, intrigue me. You help me see things differently. In brighter colours … I drew you like that because that's the way I see you."

His warm smile stroked a new colour on my pallet. A colour I didn't need to be scared of – or prepared for. For some reason it felt natural. My heart softened. I felt OK.

"The second piece of artwork I've seen by the incredible Peyton Swift."

"Second?"

"Yeah. I saw the tattoo on Liam's arm. When I came round for dinner and you were helping your mum dish out dessert, it was just the two of us in the lounge and I asked him which one you had designed."

"Sneaky."

"I have my moments … I think it's awesome by the way. How would you feel if I got one of your pieces inked on my skin? I'd prefer it to be original, a one of a kind, but whatever piece you felt was right I'd accept."

"You're going to get a tattoo?"

"I'm thinking about it, especially since I have my very own artist at my beck and call. If or when I got one, would it make me cuter, hotter and or sexier?"

I laughed.

"Seriously. Which one do you think I am?"

"Well because you said and slash or, I could think that you're more than one of the above categories."

"And in our questionnaire you answered yes to the above question, all I want to know is which one."

"N.A."

I smiled as I observed the nature surrounding me. After spending time with Kai, I found he wasn't a surfer type of guy after all. Maybe the hair threw me the first time we met, but I quickly came to realise he was a rock type of guy. A rock god. My rock god. In the sanctuary of my own thoughts I was free to admit and accept that he was hot, cute and sexy. But I wasn't going to tell him it was all three.

The air grew colder. We snuggled in the blanket and talked about travelling around the world and places we'd always wanted to go. The places we wanted to go together. We spoke about our dreams and what we had wanted to be when we were kids. Kai said he'd wanted to be an astronaut, but as he grew older he had become interested in being a paramedic. I told him I had wanted to be an artist – I still kind of did – but as I got older I turned it into a more realistic job and was fixed on being an art teacher. But now that was out of the question because I hadn't even graduated from high school. I felt like I would vomit just thinking about school.

As the days passed since returning home from hospital and my confessions with Dr Wilson, the cruel details of that moment were becoming clearer. Sharper. Deep down I knew that I wouldn't be able to run from those thoughts or ignore that part of my past for much longer. No matter how hard I tried.

The blanket and our bodies kept us warm. Glancing at Kai, I wondered what colours he saw that moment in. That day, for me, not everything was grey. And I was OK with that. We stared into each other's eyes. Our faces so close to one another. He slowly leant closer then whispered. "Can I kiss you?"

We'd already kissed before so I knew how sweet it could be, but I wished that he'd just kissed me without asking. I was also glad he did ask. It proved he cared. Proved he wanted me to be comfortable.

My curiosity hurriedly took over my doubtfulness.

I nodded. Then closed my eyes just like he did and our lips touched. At first I flinched. A part of me didn't want to continue. Kai noticed my slight restraint. For a couple of seconds he stopped. He didn't move his face from mine. I didn't move mine from his.

I wanted his kiss.

I closed my eyes and leant to him. He came back to me and we kissed again. I felt my darkness search for an entrance into my thoughts. But I ignored it. I wanted to feel the moment. Really feel. I wanted to see the colour it offered.

We slowly left each other's lips and moved backwards, staring at one another. I saw the question printed on his face, 'Did I like it?' So many things ran through my mind, but the sweet taste of his kiss lingered and I craved more. I kissed him again and hoped that was a good enough answer. Our lips moved in lusting emotion. But he still somehow kept a gentleness, and that brought relief.

I liked his kisses. I liked the light they brought.

In that moment, I liked the colours I saw.

Chapter TWENTY-EIGHT

Kai and I stayed wrapped in the blanket surrounded by the darkened bark beauty. The trees felt like our protectors. I could almost pretend that we had been immersed in a mysterious fantasy world, and in that moment we could act like we were the only two humans on earth.

In-between us chit chatting, we kissed. Each time we kissed it felt right. And somehow every kiss was better than the last.

I liked that. It felt OK for me to like it.

The sun was slowly setting. We decided to make our way back home. My heart tickled my insides as I put the helmet back on. I wondered if Kai could tell how big my smile was behind it. I sat on the bike and held onto him. I squeezed tighter as he revved the engine and we shot away.

The ride was exhilarating – just like it was before. The speed mixed with the fresh wind that whisked past our bodies made me feel like we were gliding. Floating. It reminded me of when I was younger, to the time I would skate at the ice rink, just before I'd smash to the floor. I was too young to appreciate that sweet moment of bliss due to the countless times I'd fall flat on my face and almost have my fingers sliced off. The moment of sliding over the ice didn't last long enough before I'd crash, so I vowed to Mum that I wouldn't go ice-skating again. She only took Liam and me a few times for family outings during winter, but I quickly realised what side of the rink I should be on.

As Kai and I continued, our surroundings merged from grass and cows to houses and cars. My pulse filled with adrenaline each time we raced past another vehicle. The rush was thrilling. I wanted to feel it again. I wanted to feel more.

Traffic lights were nearing. I noticed the light turning from green to amber. We were just far enough away that we could either drive on – continuing forward, continuing this feeling – or we could slow down to a stop. I wanted Kai to risk it. My heart hammered.

I realised he'd started to slow down when the cars and lines on the pavement became clear. The light was red. We stopped. I felt my adrenaline drop. All of a sudden, I felt guilty for silently pleading for him to risk running a red light. Who was I to ask him to jeopardise his life for me? Who was I to get him to do something illegal just so I could clutch onto a thrill until it vanished minutes later?

The seconds dragged before the light turned green, my guilt weighing on me. I wasn't paying attention. My sight was locked with the ground. The numbness that was slowly settling vanished when we suddenly drove off. I squeezed Kai tight. My body was buzzing again.

I felt brave.

The modern gentleman that he was, Kai walked me right to my front doorstep. Mum was on a late shift so we were safe from being caught with the "death trap" as she called them. I couldn't help but picture what Mum would have done if she had known what had happened. She probably would have asked for Kai's keys and told him to go home. Then she'd have escorted me inside, given me a short lecture on safety and question what I was thinking, and why I was taking a risk like this since I'd just been in a car crash. Then she'd keep her angry face on for thirty minutes. I knew Liam would've been impressed. Even though he's more into cars, he can appreciate a decent vehicle when he sees one. He was at his friends' house before heading back to college the next morning. I knew if he'd seen he wouldn't have told Mum. I was a little disappointed that his visit only lasted a few days – but he had to get back to his studies. I was so happy I'd seen him that I didn't want to dwell on the feeling of missing him that would soon swell to the surface.

I turned to Kai to see him ruffle his hair. "Do you want to hang out some more?"

"What about your mum?" Kai said. "I don't think I'm ready to be chased out of the house with a frying pan. I don't think I'd have enough time to casually rev up my motorbike and make my fast getaway so you still thought I was cute, hot and or sexy. So I'd have to run down the street and leave my bike stranded to fend for itself and I don't even want to think what your mum would do to my bike."

"Kai," I chuckled, "Mum won't be back for a while. She's on a late shift. And I promise I'll make sure you leave with plenty of time before she gets home. You and your bike will be safe and sound."

He took a breath. "OK then."

We cooked popcorn and decided to watch a movie. Kai told me to choose whatever I wanted. I found myself sway towards another classic black and white film. I felt as though I had experienced so many colours that day, I wasn't sure if I was ready to continue to push my boundaries. I had enjoyed the light that we shared and the colours I had seen. I didn't want to ruin it. I turned the TV on and hoped the Classic channel was playing something in black and white. An orchestra blared through the speakers. The sound of trumpets beat my eardrums. A film had just started. I felt my muscles relax as I saw no colours.

Kai and I cuddled on the sofa. After our moment together in the forest it felt right – better than right.

The credits rolled as we made out. The end music felt like we were in our own movie. Like our moment was being scored. The instrumental music reflected my joyfulness – my unexpected, almost fully fledged happiness. It made the kissing even better. When we stopped kissing, we gazed into each other's eyes. It was like his were sparkling. They were colours I could use to paint my world brighter.

Kai softly caressed my cheek then brushed my hair behind my ear. "I'm falling more in love with you, Peyton Swift."

My mind flashed with fear. Uncertainty. I couldn't say that I loved him back. He didn't actually say he loved me anyway, just that he was falling more in love with me. I didn't even know if I loved him. *Did I love him?* I liked him. *More than liked, and it was more than a crush.* I just wasn't ready to say love. Love was a word that meant so much and I didn't know if I was ready for those colours – for that light. He pecked the tip of my nose. My body tingled. Blood pumped through my veins. He was teaching me to have more courage. The thought of intimacy took over the previous stumps of doubt.

"Do you want …" I breathed. *Was I ready for that?* "Do you want to?"

"Do I want to, what?"

I just looked at him, kind of raised my eyebrows and hoped he could read my thoughts.

Kai stared at me with an expression of surprise. "Do *you* want to?"

We made our way to my room. It wasn't sexy like in the movies when they passionately roll down the walls while pashing and stripping each other of their clothes. Kai and I took slow steps together while we held hands. He held mine tightly and I was grateful. I didn't want to float away. Right in that moment he felt like my anchor.

My mind crashed with thoughts. My darkness tried to search for an entrance. But I wanted to see colours. I wanted to see light. I'd been told that being intimate was supposed to be bright. Magical. I needed to test that theory.

I opened my door, thankful I'd kind of cleaned my room the other day. It had been my room for eleven years. It wasn't supposed to be spit-spot clean – I didn't think anyway. A few clothes were sprawled on the floor and a couple of my drawers were slightly open. CDs were stacked on my shelves alongside my favourite trinkets. The smell of vanilla encompassed everything in the room.

I felt uneasy. Unprepared. But partly happy.

I looked at Kai. *Did he still want to?* I was nervous. And could tell he was too, his smile soft. We released our hands. He lingered in the doorway. I assumed he wanted another invitation.

"So, this is my room …" I stretched my arms out wide.

Kai stepped into my space.

My heart raced.

His eyes inspected my CD collection. The art scattered on my walls. "You drew all these?"

I nodded.

Some were small scraps of paper with pen sketches that I had stuck above my desk. Others were different sized painted canvases that hung on my walls. During my earlier days out of hospital I was able to haze out the colours they were cloaked with – ignore their presence. Since I'd met Kai I'd been able to accept the colours without caution. I wasn't afraid to open my eyes in the morning and look at what I had produced. I wasn't afraid to feel what I felt when I looked at them. I might not have been able to look at them for long, but it was a start. It was better than nothing.

I observed Kai as he continued to inspect my bedroom. I assumed he was finished when he turned to face me. Our eyes met. My heart skipped a beat.

Were we really going to do it? Did I want to do it?

Yes.

No.

Maybe.

No.

I swallowed the lump in my throat that was on the verge of choking me. The darkness in me was spreading. I didn't want it to, but I couldn't help it. Kai edged towards me. I slid back slightly. My mind fluttered at how attractive I found him.

"Do you still want to?" He asked. "It's OK if you don't."

I opened my mouth. My words weren't released. I coughed to clear my throat. "Um …" *Did I want to?*

Yes.

No.

Maybe.

A memory thrashed to the front of my mind. It was so forceful – my skin felt it too. I was beginning to feel repulsed by the touch Kai had not yet given me.

"Peyton, we don't have to do this if you don't want to. If you're not ready, it's fine. We can go back to the lounge and watch another movie or maybe I go home and we can hang out tomorrow…"

I pressed on one of my scabs – the largest one that brought

me the most pain. My pressured touch didn't work as well as I wanted. I didn't know what to do. Thinking about being intimate only produced hurt and pain. But I still needed to know if it could be something better. Brighter. If it was, then maybe I could move on. Maybe I could take a step in the right direction to feeling better about myself. Allowing myself to live. To love. To be. "I think I want to … Do you?"

"Only if you do." Kai took my trembling hand in his. I was almost inclined to snatch it away, but there he was – my anchor.

The darkness slightly decreased. His touch centred my fast-tracked mind. I felt ready. Or as ready as I could be.

I felt OK. I felt safe.

"I do." My heart fluttered as the words left my lips.

Suddenly, I became weary. I looked up at him and reached for a kiss so I didn't overthink. We met halfway. Our lips touched. The sensation sparked a light in me. A defence I used to fight my darkness.

It was quiet. We stepped together and settled, perched at the end of my bed. I searched his blue/brown eyes. They told me what I already knew. He was caring. Loving. Present in the moment. I hoped my eyes didn't reveal my internal battle. My worries. My doubt. My darkness.

I reached for his face and traced it with my lightly trembling hand. His skin was soft. Warm. My thumb stroked his eyebrow before my fingers combed his thick hair. He didn't move, as if he knew any sudden movement would make me retreat. I removed the thin headband he wore and dropped it to the ground. He flicked his hair then tousled it. We both smiled.

Kai's thumb gently traced my lips. I breathed slowly. I wanted to know what he thought. My mind was swept with wild thoughts. Kai leant in and kissed me. We worked our bodies into the movement. Our shoulders rolled and our fingertips kneaded each other's skin. My heart continued to race.

Kai slipped his t-shirt off. Like admiring a sculpture, I studied his physique. He wasn't chiselled like a Roman gladiator; his figure was lean and I could see the foundation of his muscles forming. He kissed me once then put his hands to my waist and lifted my jumper over my head. We panted in need for air and each other's kiss. I wore a singlet and he gently removed it, making me feel exposed. Unready. I was uneasy and questioned whether intimacy was what I wanted. His fingertips grazed the arch of my back. A memory flashed. My muscles tensed and my body jolted. I still hoped my eyes didn't reveal my internal battle.

Kai stopped and looked at me.

"It's OK. Let's keep going …" I shook the thought from my mind, reached for his face and kissed him. I tried to mean it as much as I could. I didn't want the dark to overtake me. I wanted the colours.

Kai lay me down. His hand rested behind my head until it touched the pillow. He was on top of me. Nerves continued to trickle through me. His bright eyes scanned over my skin. They found the marks. I wondered what he thought of my scabs. My scars. He touched some of my healed wounds as if he were drawing them on me. He pecked a couple of them on my forearm. "Are these from your accident?"

"Yes." I wanted to know what he was thinking. I wanted to be in his head.

He whispered. "They're beautiful."

Kai's kisses made their way up my neck. Then his lips were on my lips. Another spark of light emerged like it had on the motorbike. I wanted the adrenaline. I wanted to feel.

I could feel him becoming ready. He unbuttoned his jeans and slid them down his legs. As he did, I took off my bra. He looked at my breasts like they were made of gold – the best treasure he'd ever seen. He kissed my stomach, which made my body roll. My insides fluttered. My stomach twisted. He unbuttoned my jeans then slipped them off. We kissed again.

Kai looked into my eyes. "Are you sure?"

I bit my lip and nodded.

We each removed our underwear. Both completely naked.

I grabbed a condom from my side drawer – I'd stolen it from Liam's room one day. Kai put it on.

I ignored the darkness that fought to bombard me. I used the specks of light that emerged as a guard. I focused on the thrilling feeling. The want of intimacy. I wanted that moment to be filled with colours. I needed that moment to be soaked with light.

I felt safe with Kai. That made me believe I could be – that I deserved to be – happy. Whole. Loved. I couldn't let myself go with anyone else. It had to be with him.

Kai and I moved as one. Our rhythm was stirring and it took over my being. I let myself go. I was unguarded. We fitted together perfectly.

In that moment, my darkness drowned out and we ignited colours. Colours I never thought I'd see.

Chapter TWENTY-NINE

I skipped out on that week's therapy session. Mum was forced to work a different shift so she couldn't get me there. I know I could've asked Kai to take me, but I didn't really want him to be a part of that portion of me. I realised it was stupid because of how much I had shared with him already. But I was more than happy to try a week without therapy. To see how I would be. I assured Mum that missing one week was going to be fine. That I was fine. Because I was. It was OK not to speak with Dr Wilson, because I had begun to open up with Kai. I had shared a part of me with him that I couldn't with anyone else – and it wasn't just the physical aspect. Sure, Kai didn't know the things I had told Dr Wilson, but he knew where my secret was kept. He was giving me time to acknowledge. To think. To feel. And if I never did, that was fine. He said he didn't care about my past.

Maybe things were better kept that way.

I wanted to spend the day with Kai, but he was working and I didn't want to distract him at the coffee shop. We sent texts back and forth, so the colours from that would have to be enough.

Me: How's work?

Kai: Boring cause you're not here.

Half an hour later.

Kai: Have u been working on my tattoo art yet? Y or N.

Me: N. I didn't think u were serious about that. Plus u haven't even told me what u want!

Kai: Yes I am serious! I would like to have a Peyton Swift original somewhere on my body. And it's called using your imagination. You're the artist! I think u know me well enough to come up with something I'll like.

Fifteen minutes later.

Kai: How's the other art coming along?

Me: So-so.

Kai: Made it into the Art Cave?

Me: N.

A couple of hours later.

Kai: Now we're one, connected by fate. Our colours collide; they can be seen from space. With you I am happy, at home and safe. With you I am whole, I have found my place.

Me: XOXO

Half an hour later.

Me: This whole time I've been trying to come up with my own poem. Wanting to impress/intrigue u and I've come up with nothing! I'm awful with words that's why I draw.
Kai: Then draw me something. OXOX

I had been camped at the kitchen table, drawing. I was no longer hesitant to grab a colour and create with it – express myself with it. I had slowly run out of materials and my hands craved to use something new. To get dirty. I knew that if I wanted to keep drawing, creating, eventually I would need to get more art supplies. I would need to go into my Art Cave.

I sauntered to the door of the garage and strongly planted in front of it, like I was proving that it no longer beat me. That I could walk in there at any time.

But I didn't go in.

The remembering had begun. The details were no longer vague. It stung. My heart dropped to my stomach then rose into my mouth. I felt like I was sinking into the floor. *I wished I was.* I stumbled away. Defeated.

It won again.

Instead, I watched TV. I eased myself into the black and white cinematography.

My phone beeped.

Kai: Would u like to have dinner with my family? Y or N.

Me: Y. I would love to.

Chapter THIRTY

The next day I awoke cocooned in my blankets. I felt low. I let a small part of me hold hope that I could have gone into my cave. That I was going to go in. Deep down, I knew I wasn't ready for it, but I wanted to capture the bravery I'd felt.

During the afternoon I tried to distract myself. I stayed away from drawing and the problem of art supplies and my cave. My healing injuries no longer brought a pain intensity that was strong enough to create a distraction, so I had to search elsewhere. I cleaned the house and went for a couple of walks. Which kept my mind at bay.

I thought about Liam and the conversation we'd had. Because I didn't step into the garage, I wanted to prove that I was OK. Even if the person I was trying to convince was Liam. I had once thought the distance between us made it easier to convince him, only to realise I had to try twice as hard. That the whole time he knew something was wrong.

Even before my crash. I grabbed my phone and sent him a text.

Me: U will be pleased to know I am working on new art! X

Liam: Really?! I'm proud of u P. Keep it up & show me something new ASAP! xx

Kai picked me up in his tin can. By that time I kind of liked it and even gave it a nickname, "Tinarrhoea" – because of the rust that bordered the doors and the back gas that trailed behind after it started up. I thought the nickname suited it completely. Kai didn't really like the name, but he said he didn't care what I called it, so long as I was there with him and I felt safe.

During the drive I battled with myself. I didn't want my tainted mood to affect my first meeting with his family and the dinner we would share. I also didn't want Kai to know I had felt defeated. That my darkness could still take such a toll on me after the colours we had created. I didn't want him to worry.

We arrived at Kai's house. It was one storey with red bricks. There was a large tree in the front garden with a home-made swing roped to it. The bark was damp from the rain and the branches were leafless. I could imagine golden-brown and orange leaves scattered across the grass during autumn. Or fresh, lush, green leaves decked on the branches at summertime. I imagined the front garden in summer –

the bright green grass and colourful petals of the flowers that welcomed you as you stepped to the front door.

Kai seemed a little nervous. I was too. As we made our way to the door, I heard his younger brother and sister playing inside, laughing. Fear took a hold because I didn't know if I was ready for their colours.

The smell of onions, garlic and steam greeted us as we entered the house. I followed Kai to the lounge. The room's colours were a rich red and gold. The wooden TV cabinet and coffee table tied the space together. Family photos were framed and hung on the wall. I was overwhelmed but kept my anxiety hidden.

"Peyton, this is my mum Melissa and my stepdad Robert." Kai smiled.

"Hello." I half-heartedly waved.

"It's *so* nice to meet you, Peyton. Just call me Mel." She smiled then kissed me on the cheek. "We've heard a bit about you. It's nice to finally put a face to the name." She was in her mid to late forties. Her dyed blonde hair was tied back in a short ponytail. Her light-blue eyes shone. She seemed to be so happy meeting someone from Kai's life.

Robert had a shaved head and trimmed goatee beard. His large brown eyes looked like melted chocolate. "Hi Peyton. Just call me Rob."

"This is my little brother, Seth," Kai said as he tousled Seth's brown hair. He scampered away and collapsed near his Lego. "And this is my little sister, Isla." Kai lifted her in the air. She giggled and wrapped her legs around his waist.

"This is Peyton, are you gonna say hi?"

Isla sheepishly gazed at me. "Hi."

"Hi Isla. You've got a very pretty name."

She smiled, resting her head on Kai's shoulder.

"I've also got another little brother; he's my stepbrother and his name's Hugh. He's not here tonight though. He's with his mum," Kai said. "Maybe you'll get to meet him next time."

Mel and Rob made their way to the kitchen for the last-minute touches for dinner. Kai, Seth, Isla and I stayed in the lounge. I sat on the sofa after peering over the family photos. I watched as Kai wrestled with Seth over the same Lego piece. Seth's laughter sprang through the air. It hit me unexpectedly. The brightness made me feel exposed. But part of me couldn't help but like the feeling.

Kai swooped up Isla and plonked himself next to me. She balanced on his knee. He bounced his legs and she threw her head back laughing. I found myself smiling.

Rob announced dinner was ready. Seth and Isla ran to the kitchen. Kai held the door open and stretched out his hand to me. I reached for it like I was in an abandoned ship. As soon as our fingers linked, I felt a little better. Like I could breathe a little easier. I was back with my anchor.

The six of us sat around the dinner table. The rich smell of home-made ratatouille wafted into my nostrils. My stomach rumbled. I sat next to Kai. Our hands brushed as we each reached for our water. A rush of anxiety swept through me. My secret lodged in the front of my brain. I suddenly lost my appetite.

"So Peyton, what do you do?" Rob asked.

For a brief moment I felt like I was unable to function. I couldn't move my lips to answer his question. I couldn't formulate words. I took a slow deep breath and thought to myself: *other than once a week going to therapy and pushing away a darkness I try my hardest to forget, nothing. I do nothing at all.*

"She's an artist. I've seen several of her original pieces and can't wait to see more." Kai smiled at me before he shoved a forkful of food into his mouth.

I was relieved Kai had answered for me. Comforted that I didn't have to speak, that I had a second longer to collect myself.

"That's fantastic, Peyton. What type of art do you make?" Mel said.

"Err …" I felt my voice shake. I cleared my throat. "I love to draw. And I dabble with acrylic paints. But watercolours are my absolute favourite."

"*I* like to paint," Isla said.

"Do you? Well maybe we could make something together one day."

Isla smiled as she slid down her chair. I envied her innocence.

"Is there anything you paint in particular?" Rob said.

"Um, I don't really like to limit myself when it comes to my art. I know I'm not good at everything; everyone has their specialties. I tend to draw people. Real and imaginative. I love drawing and painting faces and eyes and I try to incorporate stories into them."

The night came to an end. I had tried my best to keep up with the conversation. To prove I was interested. As the night progressed, I couldn't ignore the haunting in my mind from my failed attempt at entering my Art Cave. It felt like a shadow was slowly taking over my brain. I pushed back at it; tried to keep that motion in the dark. But the feeling continued to crawl through my mind. Relodge at the front of my thoughts. I felt sick to my stomach. The tightening wouldn't subside.

I said goodbye to Mel and Rob. Kai's parents were really nice. I hoped they didn't see the worrying in my eyes. I was ready for Kai to take me home. Ready to be in a place I knew. As soon as we stepped outside I felt like I would be swallowed into the ground or lifted to the sky. But somehow I managed to make my way to Kai's car.

The night air was fresh and made my body tremble. But it wasn't the real reason why my bones clattered. The stars hid behind the murky clouds. I was thankful for the dark surroundings and hoped they would drown my vulnerability.

The static from the radio toured between us. The murmur of music played behind it. Kai said he'd tried to fix it, but I didn't mind. I knew he was going to spark a conversation and I was worried about how well I could hold up my end.

"So, how was dinner?" Kai said.

"Fine … It was really nice. The food was great."

"I was worried that Mum was going to bring out baby photos of me naked in the paddling pool." He laughed. "Sorry if Isla or Seth got a bit too in your face. When they like someone they tend to really ..."

"Kai, your family is lovely. Thanks for letting me meet them."

The radio continued to play up – I was glad it did. I needed a constant distraction. I hoped I could turn it into a game again. Wondering when a sound would play. Wondering what words would be said. Kai reached for a button then twisted a nozzle and the sound stuck. A song I was unfamiliar with played without static interruptions. Supposedly it was one of the hottest tracks right now, according to the host. It was a bit too repetitive for my liking.

We stopped at a set of traffic lights. The heating from the car kept me warm. I stared out at a hooded male figure walking on the footpath. He turned in my direction. It was him. It was him, the boy who stole a part of me. It was him and there was nowhere for me to run. He'd caught me again. Trapped me. It felt like our eyes locked. Remembering the hate in his eyes pierced me, I could almost taste blood. Suddenly, a flash of headlights highlighted his face, revealing a stranger. My muscles remained tense. Deep down I knew it wasn't him and I knew that stranger didn't see me. He couldn't have because of the darkness, the distance. But that didn't stop the thrust of dread. I detached my gaze and stared through the windscreen. I couldn't stop my limbs from trembling. My bones continued to rattle. Gingerly, I turned just my eyes to see that the man had continued on his stroll.

Right in that second, I wanted to be home. I wanted safety.

I wanted to feel safe. My mind rushed. I began to remember details. To acknowledge them. *There of all places.*

The traffic lights turned green. The car began to roll. I felt Kai's eyes on me.

"Peyton are you OK?"

I couldn't look at him. "Yeah. Just a little cold … and tired."

"Do you want the heat up?"

"No, it's all right. We're almost there." *Almost home.*

"You sure?"

I nodded.

My breaths were shallow. My weakening body seemed to only give strength to those thoughts. The night's sky no longer made things better. I knew that this time I wasn't going to be able to shake the feelings away. I wasn't going to be able to bury the memories. I was going to remember everything. Every moment. Every detail. And it was happening that night.

Kai and I arrived at my house. The drive wasn't fast enough. Every second felt like torture. I wanted to leave Kai's side. I couldn't have him think he was the cause for my outburst. My breakdown. We parked in the driveway.

"Thanks for tonight." I smiled the best I could. "It was great to meet your family. It'd be nice to do it again sometime." I unbuckled my seatbelt and reached for the door handle.

Kai touched my hand that was closest to him.

Reluctantly I turned to him.

"Don't I get a kiss goodnight?" He smiled sweetly.

I didn't want to kiss him. Not when I was like this.

He leant to me. Our lips locked but I didn't like the taste. I didn't feel the passion. His hand moved from the back of my neck and slipped over my breast. His fingers trailed down towards my waist. I stopped the kiss and retreated. I pushed him away.

"No." I wiped my mouth.

"What's wrong?" Kai's face was a picture of concern. "Peyton?"

He reached his hands towards me.

I knew they were holding comfort but I slapped them away. "*No.* Stop. Get *away* from me!" I escaped the car and ran to the front door.

Kai rushed behind me. "Peyton, what's going *on?*"

My throat swelled. My vision blurred. I reached for the door handle. Clutched onto it as if that was my anchor. I turned to face him, to prove I meant what I was about to say "*Stay away* from me! Leave me *alone!*" I stumbled inside. Slammed the door and locked it.

Kai knocked. I heard him call for me. But I wasn't going to respond. I couldn't.

I rushed to my room.

Chapter THIRTY-ONE

I was home alone. The small fraction of me that still felt happiness was relieved that Mum was at work. I wouldn't have been able to fake it. I wouldn't have been able to convince her I was anything other than disheartened.

I landed on my bed. Tears fell down my chin. *I was remembering everything.* I didn't have a choice. I didn't have a chance to cease the memories. To halt their presence. It was too late.

It felt like the world's water rushed over my body. I was losing oxygen fast. I closed my eyes and tried to shut it all off, but the flashing memories sparked through my mind. I saw it. I felt it. Skin. Screaming. Begging. Pleading. Blood trickling. His hands locked around my wrists, holding me in place. His black stare piercing my soul. His heavy breaths as he forced himself into me. I opened my eyes but didn't find relief. I still saw it. I still felt it. Pain.

I was breaking.

I could no longer hear Kai calling out to me. I could no

longer hear the knocking on the front door. Not that I was going to let him in. I didn't want him to see me like this. I couldn't let him see me like this.

It was morning. My eyes cracked open. I woke with dry eyes. *Had I used up all my tears?* Somehow I had slept. I woke up with a small fighting chance of hope. *But what was the point?*

My phone beeped.

The echo made me jolt. I almost released a scream.

I knew who it was. I looked at the screen and saw eight unread texts.

Kai: Peyton what's going on? *8:59 pm*

Kai: Please open the door. *9:02 pm*

Kai: I'm going home now. Let me know if u need anything. OXOX *9:33 pm*

Kai: Talk to me. Let me help. *10:27 pm*

Kai: Please call me. *11:00 pm*

Kai: Did I do something wrong? *11:13 pm*

Kai: Do you hate me? *11:15 pm*

Kai: Peyton, this is breaking my heart. Please respond to my messages. *7:14 am*

I didn't respond to any of them. I couldn't. That would only encourage him to drive to my house and plea for an audience with me. I couldn't have him here. I couldn't handle him here. *I couldn't handle what had happened.*

It was afternoon. I fell asleep, drained of everything. I needed rest. I woke knowing I had to cut Kai off. Cut him off completely. I didn't want to drag him through the mud with me. A guy like him shouldn't have to put up with someone like me. Especially given his past with his father. I knew it was best if I just ignored him. Let him forget about me.

My phone beeped.

I ignored it.

Minutes passed and it beeped again. I couldn't take the risk of not reading the message. It could have been Mum or Liam. I could tell Mum knew there was something going on. That morning I had kept my distance from her. I had locked myself in my room and told her my creative juices were flowing. That I was creating a masterpiece and needed space. The truth was, I was crumpled on the other side of the door with my back against it – ready to push if she tried to open it. The truth was, I couldn't bear to look at her. I couldn't look at her beautiful face or be around her kindness. I couldn't look her in the eye, as I was drenched in the remembrance of my darkness. I wasn't strong enough to mask myself with bravery. My armour was broken and I knew she would see through the cracks too easily.

Mum had sent me a message earlier that read: "I love you. XX"

I knew she loved me. We liked to send random messages

to one another – it was a Swift-family thing. But that day, her three-worded text felt like it was coming from a different place. Maybe because I was in a different place.

The text wasn't from Mum or Liam, it was from Kai.

Kai: Can I come over? Y or N.

I waited several minutes before I replied. I knew my response would bring him disappointment.

Me: N.

He replied immediately.

Kai: Why?

I wiped the tears that fell down my chin.

Me: N.A.

Don't hate me.

The house was soaked in silence. The dull sound of the ticking clock was all I heard. I stood in the lounge, compulsively staring at the air in front of me. I couldn't shake away my past. My long dark hair drooped over me. I felt like a creepy-zombie-girl from a horror movie. My body swayed. I didn't stop the movement. It kind of soothed me.

My phone beeped.

I knew it was Kai. This time, I didn't even check it.

In the middle of the lounge, my eyelids grew heavy and my thoughts were searing. Every heartbeat hurt with the moments leading up to the accident. The details of my secret. My pain. The reason why I forced myself to see grey.

I found myself in front of the door. The door that led to my artwork. My fingers trembled as I reached for the handle. It felt like ice against my skin. I opened the door and moved inside. The strong aroma of paint and pencil sharpenings attacked my nose. My hand found the light switch. My teary eyes searched the space. It was exactly how I had left it. Exactly how I remembered. Two large tables were filled with art supplies and pieces I had been working on. Shelves were stacked with new stock. The overhead light brightened the room. It used to make me feel warm – safe – but in that moment it was just a light. Something for me to see my past with.

I warily stepped towards the canvases at the easel. There were three. The largest was displayed on the wooden stand and the other two leant against the legs. I glared at the paint-stained squares. It felt like I had been shot in the chest.

One canvas was attacked with red paint splattered one layer upon another.

The image on the second canvas was a giant eye. My

eye. Blue like the dark layer of the ocean and detailed with patterns showcasing the bloodshot. The eyelids were raw. Crystal-like tears filled the brim and looked like they were about to descend onto the floor, leaving a large puddle that would need to be mopped up. Over the eye were messily painted words, written thin enough that the detailing of the eye colour, and the hurt it embodied, shone past them. The words read everything I had been feeling. Everything I am feeling: Broken. Vulnerable. Lost.

The third canvas was the largest of the three. It sat on the arms of the easel. As I examined the piece, a horrid taste filled my mouth. It was the portrait of a boy. *The* boy. His face was drawn from an angle so you wouldn't know it was him, unless you really knew him. I knew it was him. *I hated him.* I had painted his dark eyes the way I remembered them. The way his jaw clenched looked like it could cut you. His face was painted decoratively and aesthetically pleasing – and I hated that I had made it look that way: as if someone could actually find it – him – pleasant. Good. Covering the canvas were paint-written words. All honest. All true. The words read: You Hurt Me. Evil. Thief.

I studied the three paintings. All my thoughts, all my feelings swirled into one. I felt like I was being taken over by a hurricane of raw emotion. I hated myself. I hated what I had become. I knew the moment I stepped into my Art Cave I would feel darker. Glummer. That was something I couldn't change. I left the cave and curled onto my bed with my dark hair wrapped around me. I was misplaced. Disorientated.

A couple of days passed. I still hadn't spoken with Kai. He had left me messages. But I'd never responded. He had come around when Mum was home. I'd told her not to let him in. She obeyed my orders.

I missed him.

The dark flashes repeated. But now there was no pause button. They continued to haunt. I was submerged in gloom. Alone.

I kept my conversations with Mum short and simple. Even the other morning when she made us waffles for breakfast. She decorated mine with a smiley face made with raspberries. From the look in her eyes I knew she didn't believe my smile.

We sat opposite each at the table. I could barely look at her.

"Peyton, sweetheart, what's wrong? What's going on? You've been …"

"I've just got a bit of a headache, Mum. That's all. I'll just drink more water or take some pain medication and I'll be fine."

"Do you need me to call Dr Enderson? Is the headache because of the crash? Because you know …"

"I know. He said I'd get terrible headaches for a little while." I shoved a forkful of waffle in my mouth and regretted it, knowing I'd have to swallow it.

"Well you better get to work, Mum. Don't want to be late. I can clean the dishes. I've got other stuff to do today anyway … I'm going to go brush my teeth now." I quickly stepped to her, barely pecked her cheek before I rushed down the hallway. I only just made it to the bathroom before tears streamed down my chin. I grabbed my towel and covered my face to mask the sound of my cries.

I knew I was pushing people away. But I didn't know what else to do. When Liam called I didn't answer. When he texted me I hardly ever replied with more than a few words. I knew I was doing the opposite of convincing him I was OK, but I didn't have the energy to play that game anymore. I could tell Mum was hurting. Consumed with worry.

I was shutting down.

I was losing my way.

Again.

Mum had tried to give me space. Let me have my time. I knew she hadn't pushed to get answers from me because usually I found my own way to her. Usually I tell her anything. I saw her concern growing.

One morning, she gently entered my bedroom. I didn't fight it. I didn't force her to leave like I had previously. I stayed covered in my bed – as if my blanket was my shield.

"Morning P." She softly sat next to me and stroked my hair. "I know something's going on. It's not a headache, and I'm not fully convinced your creative juices have been flowing. Peyton, sweetheart. *Talk* to me. Let me help you. What's going on?"

I couldn't say anything. I didn't want any more tears. But I felt them piling up my tear ducts.

"Is it to do with Kai? Did he *hurt* you?"

"No." I sniffled. "It's not about him."

I could tell she was fighting back her own tears. Trying to be strong. "Is it to do with the accident?"

I nodded. Tears roll down my cheeks.

"P, if you don't want to speak to *me* about it, it's OK. I understand. But I really think you should try and speak with Dr Wilson … You like him, don't you? He's been helping …" She kissed the top of my head then rested her chin on my hair as she whispered almost inaudibly: "I don't want to lose you." She kissed my head again.

I didn't want to be lost.

I agreed to speak with Dr Wilson. I told her he was the only person I wanted to talk to, even though I knew that would hurt her. He was the only person I could talk to. I didn't know why. Maybe his office was my sanctuary.

Chapter THIRTY-TWO

I crumbled in my usual cream chair, with Dr Wilson opposite me. I sat there with full acknowledgement of my past. Full recognition of the details of my secret. The discomfort expanded. I couldn't change it. "I think I should go."

"You've only just arrived, Peyton."

A rich silence fell. I rose from the chair without another word. Without another glance at his grey eyes. I shuffled to the door. Then froze. I stared at the handle. Something inside me made me stop. A tear rolled down my cheek. My breath became congested. My shoulders dropped. The words spilt from my lips. "I remember … I remember everything … the details about when I was … raped."

I turned to Dr Wilson. The look on his face said so much, but I didn't let that stop me.

"I know all the reasons for my darkness and my car crash. Because of what happened, I stopped making art. Because of what happened, I am who I am now. Lost. Guarded. Broken." I wiped another tear that fell to my chin. "Nobody else knows. I couldn't tell *anyone*. Not even after I told you … I didn't want to tell anyone. I *never* wanted to share this. Not even with my mum. In fact, *especially* not her. I wanted to keep it a secret forever. I was embarrassed. I *am* embarrassed. I keep questioning why it happened to me, but I just don't know."

I took a scattered breath and hoped that would recharge my courage. "The memories play in my mind, constantly on repeat. It had been a month and still they never stopped. They never left me. Even when I slept they crept through my brain. I'd wake up drenched in sweat. I'd shower, clean myself up but I still felt dirty. Like I'd bathed in mud. I would scrub my skin until I was raw. Until I felt something other than sadness. I dyed my hair darker so I didn't look the same. I crawled back into my shell …

"Hours before the crash I sat on my bed. I could still feel his fingers force their way over my body, my neck, my breasts, my hips. I closed my eyes and I could see everything. I jolted my body around as if he were there with me. He wasn't. I was alone. But I still remembered everything, every second.

"The school day had ended. I'd stayed behind to clean up my desk. My art teacher and I had a good relationship; she trusted me not to steal anything and to close the door when I left. That day, the boy came into the room. He made his way to the windows and closed all the blinds. I asked what he was doing and he pretended he was interested in me; he pretended he was interested in my art. He said that he was jealous of how creative I was. How gifted I was with pencils and brushes. As he spoke he roamed around the room then he closed the door, locked it and edged a chair under the handle. I asked what was going on and without a second thought he said he wanted to fuck me to next Tuesday. I tried to leave. He jumped over tables to grab me. I screamed but everyone had left. I asked him to let me go. But he wouldn't have any of it. He told me he and his friends had made a bet about who would take my virginity away. He said he had to win. He wanted to win no matter what. He pinned me down on a table. His fingers pressed every part of my body. He shoved his hand up my dress and ripped my underwear off, in between forcing my lips open."

My first kiss.

"I hit him. I *tried* to make him stop but he was so much stronger than me. He knew his way around a girl's body and started doing what he wanted. I lay on the table with his large hand locked around both of my wrists; he held my arms above my head. I was like a piece of paper pinned to a board. I twisted and tried to slip from his hold but it didn't help. His fingers rushed down my squirming body until they were deep inside me. He forced them in and it burned. Tears fell down my cheeks as he roughly moved his fingers around trying to get me ready. I begged him to stop.

"He removed his fingers and sat on top of me, taking one wrist in each hand and kept them over my head. I looked him right in the eyes and *pleaded* for him to stop. I promised I wouldn't tell *anyone* if he stopped right then. He replied by leaning over my face and roughly locking his lips on mine.

I bit his lip and drew blood. It trickled down his chin. He called me a bitch but I could tell in his sick twisted way he liked it. I could feel him getting harder and I knew what was coming next … He was still on top of me. His weight heavy over me. He said 'I promise you'll like it.' Words of protest wouldn't leave my mouth. I couldn't move. I felt like I couldn't breathe.

"He was inside me and it hurt, but I still couldn't make a sound. He rocked until he was finished. Then he quickly zipped his trousers up. 'Thanks for the memories,' he said, and left.

"I dropped to the floor in shock. My wrist had cracked but it wasn't broken. My elbows throbbed as they wacked the ground. I covered myself with my arms. I felt naked. Tears streamed down my face. I was alone. Left with silence. I quickly grabbed my things and ran from the school, not wanting to believe what had happened.

"I raced home. Every sudden sound made me jump. I rushed to my room, ignoring everything as I went. Mum asked me how my day was and I told her it was fine. I promised myself right then I wasn't going to tell *anyone*. I couldn't tell anyone … It would show how weak I was. How weak I *am*.

"I sat on the shower floor and let the water trickle down my back as I sobbed. I couldn't stop the tears. My skin felt like it was layered in his fingerprints, like they had been tattooed all over my body. Forever marked by his touch. I dropped out of school because I couldn't stand to be in the same place as him, breathing the same air. I couldn't stand the way he looked at me in the corridors. He looked at me like I had been conquered. And that he'd do it again.

"My grades weren't the best and school was never my favourite place to be. Art class was the only reason I attended. It was the only pleasure I got out of school. I didn't really have any friends. I had no one to say goodbye to. Leaving that place wasn't hard. In fact it was easy. It didn't take too much convincing for my mum – we'd spoken about me dropping out of school a couple of times before – but I know she never thought I would actually go through with it."

I glanced at Dr Wilson to see if he was still with me. I didn't want to pause too long. Otherwise I knew I wouldn't continue with my confession. My feet were planted on the floor. My chest throbbed. I tried to keep tall but every part of me felt weak. Through my teary eyes I saw that he was still listening. I found the same spot in the room I'd been focusing on.

"I wanted to be in that crash … I didn't plan it. It just happened. The crash was my escape. Or a cry for help I guess. I know I shouldn't have been driving by myself because I only had my learner's permit, but I wanted to risk it. I had to … My skin still stung with his fingerprints. All I wanted was to escape him and what he did. I was driving, lost in myself. I looked ahead and pictured him in the middle of the road, just metres in front of me. He looked like I had painted him and the water colours were dripping down his body. Without thinking twice, I weighted my foot on the pedal. The engine roared. I kept my sight on him. The road was empty. It was just the two of us. I imagined him running away, heading for the bridge. But I lost sight of him when the car swerved, and I panicked. He flashed in front of the windshield. I pointed the car towards him. I knew what I was doing as I crashed into the bricks. I pretended I had broken his bones, that I had shattered his soul like he did mine … I wanted him to feel *my* pain.

"I knew it was just a figment of my imagination. But I didn't want to stay here if I would always feel weak and used. I was exposed. *He* exposed me. He *broke* me. I didn't want to stay that way. I don't want to stay that way."

There it was. My darkness. My secrets. My past out in the open. Somebody else knew all the details. It was out, in the light.

I felt tired. Heavy. I stepped towards the cream chair and only just landed in it. Dr Wilson's eyes followed me but he didn't speak. *He must have been waiting to see if there was anything else I had to say.*

There were no more words. Only tears.

Chapter THIRTY-THREE

A couple of days had passed. My darkness was still a big part of me, but I felt lighter. I continued to ignore Kai's texts. I didn't want to be around him. I couldn't handle his colours. His light. Even the thought of it became too much. I knew ignoring someone who had given themselves to me physically and emotionally was unkind. I never wanted to be that type of person, but I thought it was for the best.

I curled on the sofa. The TV was off. I was left with myself. Left with my thoughts. It might not have been the wisest choice, but I wasn't ready for a colourful, drama-filled distraction or a black and white one. I just wanted to fade away. I wanted to forget.

My phone beeped.

I unlocked it and read the text.

Kai: Just tell me if u hate me. Just give me that answer and if u do I'll leave u alone. U won't hear from me again. U won't have to see me again. Just please let me know.

My heart hurt. I knew how much I was hurting him. *I should never have let things go that far.* I replied to his message. It felt like forever since I had.

Me: I don't hate you, Kai. I don't think I ever could.

I wanted him to reply instantly – like the way he used to. Two minutes passed and there was still nothing. My heartstrings pleaded for a little poem. A single word.

Something.

Anything.

"Then why are you ignoring me, Peyton Swift?!" Kai's voice entered my ears.

I stretched out my legs and pushed myself to sit up. My eyes widened. My stomach convulsed. He was there. Outside my house. I was trapped. I knew he wouldn't leave without seeing me – he wouldn't leave without speaking to me. Not until he understood my harsh departure from his world.

I pulled the curtain and peered through the window. He caught me. For a couple of seconds our eyes locked. I swept the curtain closed and dropped to the floor.

"Peyton?"

I took slow deep breaths and rose from the floor. I stepped towards the front door. *I knew I had to face him.* He wouldn't leave otherwise. I tried to let my breaths soothe my voice. Calm my thoughts.

Kai knocked at the door. The sound made me jump.

"Peyton *please* open up. I know you're in there. *Please* just talk to me."

My hands trembled as I unlocked the door. I wasn't scared. *I was nervous.* Unprepared for what was about to happen. Slowly I opened the door. There he was – jeans and a jumper, his hair almost touching his shoulders. There he was, waiting for me. Patient. Kind. His face painted with a mix of worry and relief. His eyes about to collect tears.

Dread pulsed through my chest. *What was I supposed say? What was I supposed to do?* I didn't think Kai knew what to say either. I assumed he'd thought he wouldn't get as far as he had. He probably thought he wouldn't even see me.

I licked my lips. "Hi."

"Hi? You put me through this shit and just say *hi?*"

What I had done wasn't fair. He had every right to be angry. He had every right to be mad. Upset. Hurt.

"Peyton, what's going on? What happened? What did I do wrong?"

"Nothing … You did nothing wrong."

"Then what happened? What's going on?"

"I didn't want to tell you … I don't know if I want to tell you."

"Don't want to tell me *what?* You can tell me *anything.* Everything."

I shook my head.

"Yes you *can.* When you're hurting, I am too. When you're upset, I am too. We're *supposed* to share things so we can help each other through our hard times. Let me *help.*"

"Not this one, Kai."

"Why?"

I hid behind my walls in my final attempts to protect myself, and him. I kept trying to push him away. *It felt like the right thing to do.*

"Why do you *care*?"

Kai's face scrunched up like a piece of paper. "What?"

I took a quick breath. "I said, why do you *care*? Just *leave* me alone. You said you were going in your text. So do *it* now."

"Is that what you *want*?"

No.

"Is it?"

"Yes."

"Fine! Whatever, Peyton. *Obviously* you never cared about me, that's why it's so *easy* for you to ignore *all* my messages, *all* my calls. Forget *it*. Forget *me*!" Kai turned and stormed to his car.

My heart cracked. Tears wouldn't fall. I lingered in the doorway. I stayed.

"You know what? *Screw* this!" Kai twirled around, and continued speaking loudly. I was ready for a neighbour to make an appearance to see what the commotion was about. "*Forgive* me if I'm concerned over the people I care about!"

"Kai …"

"What? You don't *believe* me? Peyton, all this time we've spent together and you still haven't grasped the concept of how I feel about you? If you haven't, then you don't know me at all."

"Kai I … I'm scared."

"It's fine to be scared. Just don't push away the people who *care* about you."

"It's not as easy as that."

"Then tell me what it is …"

I bit my lip until it hurt.

"Peyton, please … You're my girlfriend. I *love* you."

I opened my mouth but no words followed.

"Got a problem with that?" Kai said.

"No."

"Good."

"I … I love you too." The words rolled from my tongue. I did love him. That was why I had tried to let him go.

My frozen tears fell. The iciness could've stung my skin if I'd let it. But I wiped them away instead. Kai stared at me with relief and confusion.

I had to tell him now. I felt like he had to know about my past. I felt like we couldn't move forward if I didn't tell him. He had to know my secret. I knew my confession would be the real test of his affections. My confession would make us or break us.

"Come inside." I took his hand.

We made our way to the lounge and sat on the sofa. Our teary eyes locked on one another. He kept his hold on my hand. I sensed that he was scared to let me go, in fear I'd run from him again. I smiled at him as warmly as I could. I wanted him to know I wasn't going to run. Not this time. I hoped he believed me.

"Kai." My tear ducts refilled. "What I'm going to say is hard. And the reason I didn't want to tell you, the reason I *don't* want to tell you, is because I'm scared that you're not going to want me anymore. That you're not going to love me anymore. That you'll look at me differently. And I *don't* want you to. I don't think I can handle it if you do."

Kai raised my hand to his lips and gently kissed my knuckles. His touch gave me a dose of strength. "You can say whatever it is."

"Promise me you'll just listen. You won't interrupt or force things that I might not be ready for … Just let me say it all before you speak."

He looked at me, confused.

"You'll understand when I'm telling you. Just please promise me that."

Kai nodded. "I promise."

I released my hand from his. I slid back a little so we weren't so close. Kai watched my movements. I took several deep breaths. "A little while ago, when I was still at school, I stayed behind in art class to clean my work station. Another student came into the room and suddenly started closing the blinds. Then, he locked door." I dropped my sight to my knees and closed my eyes. I licked my lips. My limbs trembled. I took a scattered breath, partly unsure if the next words would leave my lips. "He raped me."

I breathed in and looked at Kai. His jaw was clenched. I knew once I had admitted everything during my therapy session it would make it a little easier to tell Kai – if I were ever going to tell him. But it was never going to hurt less when the words left my lips. It was never going to minimise my fear that he would never want to see me again.

"That's the reason I dropped out of school. I couldn't handle seeing him, being near him. That's the reason I crashed the car. All my memories were dark, soaked with the way he made me feel. I didn't want to live like that anymore … The night I was driving, my mind was distracted. I swerved and I remember panicking. But I didn't care if I was going to crash. Afterwards the injuries made me feel a little better, because I could feel physical pain. All the other pain was inside my head. I felt better having wounds on the outside, because people could see I was injured. That I was hurting."

I watched as Kai's face changed. The thing I didn't want the most had happened. *Were the colours he saw me in fading?*

I took Kai's hand and led him down the hall. He followed me willingly. Without question. Although I had requested his silence, it made me hurt. I wanted to know the thoughts that ran through his mind. I wanted to know what he thought about me now. My free hand slightly trembled as I touched the door handle. I squeezed Kai's hand and hoped his touch would offer me more strength. I opened the door. Kai had been my anchor, and I knew right then I had to be his. Even if that was the last time we would be together. Even if that was the last time I would see his eyes. I switched the light on. We stepped into the room.

"Kai Pearson, welcome to my Art Cave."

Welcome to the place that I hid my secret.

I directed him towards the easel. Towards the three canvases where I had expressed my secret. Where I had expressed my hurt. My anger. My truths. We stood in front of the paintings. I didn't let go of his hand. He didn't even attempt to let go of mine. I forced myself to remember what it felt like when we held hands. Because a part of me believed it was the last time we would be. I gazed up at him. His eyes scanned my art. His eyes examined my work. They saw my hurt. My pain. My darkness.

"These are what I made after it happened."

Kai studied them. He still hadn't said a word since I had made him promise to just listen.

"Um, you can say something now, if you want to …" My eyes remained locked on him. His lips slowly opened. I was ready for his words to exit his mouth. In that moment I didn't care what they were. I just wanted to hear his voice.

"They're so honest."

I tried to settle my fast heart. "That's why I couldn't come in here … I tried my *hardest* to forget what happened. I tried my hardest to ignore the hurt. Then the crash happened and I couldn't help but think it was a gift, because that part of my past was a little blurred. But it didn't take long for the nightmares to kick in and for me to remember it again. Every time I shook them from my mind, until I couldn't shake them anymore."

"You remembered everything when we kissed in the car and I touched you?"

I nodded.

"I'm sorry."

"No Kai, it's not your fault. I remembered what happened *before* that night, it's just that I couldn't hide away from it anymore. And remembering everything was going to happen no matter what, no matter where I was."

Kai stared back at the paintings. "And you went to therapy instead of doing art?"

"Yes and no. The doctor thought it might help talking about things."

"The doctor *knew*?"

"No. He wanted me to talk about the crash. He didn't know there were other things involved." *At least I didn't think he did.*

"And that's the guy who ..." Kai nodded at the portrait with his whole body clenched. He asked the question I didn't want him to.

I continued to look at him. Hoped my constant stare would avert his attention towards me. But his eyes didn't leave that canvas. "Yeah."

"Have you told the police? The school? Any ..." Kai stopped himself. He must have remembered the promise. He turned to me. Our eyes met.

Was that it? Were we finished? Did he hate me now?

"Thank you," Kai said.

I bit my lip. Tried to hold back the sobs I felt growing.

"Thank you for telling me. Thank you for trusting me, for letting me see your darkness. Thank you for letting me into your Art Cave, for showing me this art … But most of all, thank you for letting me love you and for loving me."

I burst into tears. Without hesitating, he wrapped his arms around me. I fell to his chest. Our hearts crashed into one another.

"Do you still love me?"

"More than anything," Kai whispered. He kissed the top of my head. "What happened to you doesn't change the way I feel about you."

Tears rolled down my chin.

The next morning I crawled into Mum's bed. I knew I had to tell her. I felt like she had a right to know. I hated keeping things from her. She was my confidante. A part of my heart. I knew telling Mum was going to be different. More difficult because I knew she would take action. We would be going to the police station; we would be pressing charges and my old school would be informed. I would have to share my state with strangers. Share what had embarrassed and hurt me for so long.

Mum and I snuggled under the blankets. I took a deep breath and looked into her bright eyes. "Mum I need to tell you something …"

"What is it?"

"I didn't want to keep it from you. I just didn't know what else to do. Please don't hate me."

"Peyton sweetheart, I could *never* hate you. And you know

you can tell me anything. You're kind of scaring me, what's happened?"

"Um, can you promise that you won't interrupt? That you'll just listen. If you don't I don't know if I can get through this."

Mum nodded. Worry overtook her.

"I meant to crash the car. I mean, I didn't *mean* for it to happen. I didn't plan it. It's just … I wanted to escape what happened to me before I dropped out of school. Mum … I was raped by a boy at school."

Her face fell with shock.

"There was nothing I could do to stop him. I tried … I tried so hard but …" I controlled my breaths. "I didn't want to tell you because I was ashamed and I didn't … I didn't want to believe that it had happened. I hardly ever spoke to him, Mum. What did I do wrong? Why did he do that?"

"Sweetheart, you did *nothing* wrong. Do not blame yourself … Oh Peyton, what can I do? What can I say to make this better?"

I needed to know she still loved me. That I was going to be OK.

Our tears fell to the pillowcases. She pulled me close, wrapped her arms around me and held me tight. For mere seconds I grasped onto the innocence I had been craving. In that moment I felt like a kid again. Like when little me fell face first and scraped her skin in a rollerblading accident, and the only thing that could make me feel better – after first aid was applied – was my mum's embrace.

I don't remember how long we stayed there. I don't remember how long we were covered in her blankets, but I was relieved I'd finally told her.

Chapter THIRTY-FOUR

I rested in the cream chair. The room hadn't changed since the first time I was there. The same light floral aroma floated through the air. The neutral tones made me feel safe.

"How are you feeling today, Peyton?" Dr Wilson said.

"I'm good … really good." I was. "How are you?"

"I'm well, thank you."

Dr Wilson never forced me to talk about something I wasn't ready to. Even after I told him my secret, his calming nature never changed.

"I told my mum and that boy I've been seeing. I told them about what happened to me."

"Peyton, that's excellent news. How does that make you feel?"

"I was scared to tell them. It was a risk. I knew that. But I found it somewhere in me to take the chance … They still love me, and now I know that I feel at ease. I feel better than OK."

"That's wonderful to hear."

"You were right, you know."

"About what?" Dr Wilson asked.

"About how telling you first would make it easier to tell others."

"I'm very glad you were able to share that part of you – with me *and* two of the most important people in your life."

Me too.

"Thank you."

Dr Wilson smiled at me. His grey eyes glittered.

"I showed someone my Art Cave and the artwork inside. The art that I was hiding from."

"Would you like to discuss that? The art you created?"

"It's honest and heartbreaking. That's why I couldn't go in there. But now I feel strong enough for it … I've been in a couple of times now. Once by myself before I told you everything, and the second time to show that someone my secret, so they understood it and me a little better."

"Do you think now that you've expressed this story, now that you've exposed this part of your life, you'll be going into your Art Cave more often and creating something new?"

"Yeah."

I liked to think so.

"And this art you've created about that part of your life, what do you plan to do with it?"

I hadn't thought about that. The canvases were just there. They were always just there. Creating them helped get the truth out of me. It also helped me share that part of my past. I hadn't made any plans to do anything with them.

"I'm not sure … I actually hadn't thought about that yet. What about you? Have you got another drawing for me?"

"Why as a matter of fact I do." Dr Wilson leant to collect a notebook. "And will I ever get to see some of your artwork?"

"Maybe at our next session. If I remember to bring something."

"I look forward to it."

At home I felt the light growing, slowly overtaking the grey. I wasn't scared anymore, knowing I had nothing to hide.

Mum and I snuggled on the sofa with a blanket wrapped over our legs. We watched one of our favourite romantic comedies. We had seen it so often we knew it line by line. It almost felt like we had actually written the script. After designating each other several characters, we spoke when it was our turn – in-between stuffing our faces with popcorn and chocolate. We wore our pyjamas and it felt like any other night. I was glad Mum treated me no differently. After I told her, I prepared myself for her to retreat to acting like I was a china doll. But she didn't. She never once looked at me like I was fragile or weak. That made me feel stronger. It reminded me that I was going to be the victor, not the victim.

I curled up on my bed. Breathed deeply. The smell of vanilla locked in my nose. I glanced over my art and the slightly messy state of my room. The space felt like my sanctuary again. I could rest in there and no longer feel defeated. I no longer felt alone. It was once the place I recognised it as – my safe place.

My phone beeped.

I read the message.

Kai: How was ur day?

Me: Good. Mum and I just finished acting out one of our favourite movies (while it was playing – we're not that weird!) Liam called so we chatted with him for a little bit. How was work?

Kai: Boring because u weren't there.

I smiled.

Me: Are u working tomorrow?

Kai: Y.

Me: Does Kai Pearson want Peyton Swift to visit him on his lunch break? Y or N.

Kai: Y.

Me: Meet at our picnic table?

Kai: Y.

I chuckled.

My phone beeped again.

Kai: I'll bring the hot chocolates.

Me: I'll bring the blanket. XOXO

Kai: Sweet dreams, Peyton Swift. Dream a little dream of me. OXOX

Chapter THIRTY-FIVE

I strolled towards the coffee shop. The sky was brighter. The air wasn't so cold. The seasons were changing. Spring was in the air. I could almost taste it.

My first walk after being out of hospital now felt like so long ago. I used to stare at the stopwatch and count the minutes I was able to survive on the outside, around other people. I couldn't help but feel like this day, this walk, was a breeze. I was happy. Content. Cleansed.

That part of my past would never be erased. It couldn't be. It could never be forgotten. But I was learning to deal with it. I had Mum and Kai to thank for that.

I waited for Kai at our picnic table. I folded the blanket like I had before, even though there was no rain on the table. A light mist of grey scattered over my surroundings. But I saw colours seeping to the foreground. I was in my own world. I breathed. My breaths lightened me. I felt calm. At ease.

The sound of Kai's voice made me whip my head around a little too quickly. "One marshmallow hot chocolate for you."

He handed me the takeaway cup. I took a sip. The sweetness hit my tastebuds. Kai plonked next to me. We leant close to one another and kissed. His kisses hadn't changed. *I still liked them.* The way he looked at me with his beautiful eyes hadn't changed. I still felt the warmth of a sunset when our eyes locked. *Every day I was falling more in love with him.* And I knew it was OK to. I deserve it. I'm worth it.

We spent his lunch break together discussing potential future travel plans and our dream destinations. We both instantly agreed to visit London to see Big Ben and have tea with the Queen. For as long as I can remember, visiting the Louvre was something I'd dreamt of doing. Kai had started arranging a scheme for when we were in Paris, to spend the night at the Louvre. I played along, not that I would actually go through with it – even though some of his ideas were quite riveting – like cramming into bins or me somehow replicating a painting on our clothes so we'd blend in with an artwork.

I told him to come round to my house later that day so we could hang out. Because I wanted to see him. I wanted to be around him. I wanted to be with him and I knew he wanted to be with me. He wasn't put off by my past. He wasn't afraid to stay.

At home I stared in the mirror. Scanned my soft skin and smiled at myself for the first time in a long time. Luckily I had no deep scarring from the accident on my face. My fingertips felt the scar near my hairline, but that was easily covered up. There were prominent scars on my arms. I liked when Kai kissed them. When I'd touch the ones on my legs, they reminded me that I was alive. *I knew that was what I wanted.* I traced their designs like I was painting them. *My scars are beautiful.*

I ran my fingers through my hair. I knew I was ready. Ready to cut it. Ready for that change. The long waves didn't feel like mine anymore. The dark strands hung around my body and I felt like they were going to strangle me in my sleep. I told Mum I wanted to change it and she bought what we needed.

She put music on. Even though we played some of our favourite songs that we'd played countless times before, it was like I was listening to them for the first time. We camped on chairs in the kitchen and talked about a new style. I had rarely been to a hairdresser, Mum was always the one to cut my hair. I told her what style I wanted and within minutes she began cutting my locks. She gave it a big trim then mixed the hair dye. The strong smell took over the house but we didn't care. The music continued to play. I was happy with the light it brought. Mum brushed my hair with the dye. After it was washed out, she cut my hair to the style I wanted.

I strutted to the bathroom, turned the light on and examined Mum's work. A large smile stretched across my face. My lighter brown hair was shoulder length and felt so soft. I flicked it around like I was in some sort of shampoo commercial. *I loved it.* It felt like another weight had been lifted from my body, like I could breathe easier.

The doorbell rang. I knew it was Kai, but looked through the peephole anyway. He had come straight to my house from the coffee shop. I knew he had because he wore his usual all-black uniform and I smelt coffee through the door. I opened it. His cheeky smile stretched across his face.

"Hey, come in."

Kai stepped inside. He hugged me tight then softly kissed my lips. "I'm liking the new hair."

"Thanks." I smiled.

"When did you do that?"

"Pretty much as soon as I got home from our lunch date."

"It looks good."

I held my smile. I was glad he liked it.

"So, do we have anything planned for tonight? Will we be watching those rich bitches again?"

"No. I'm not really in the mood for their drama … How about creating some art?"

Kai smiled. His eyes beamed.

We made our way into my Art Cave.

"I expect to see great things from you, Mr Pearson."

"Art's not my strong suit, Miss Swift."

No, words are.

"But for you, I'll try. And don't get all jealous if what I end up creating becomes this *mega* masterpiece that has the art critics and the entire world raving about my talent."

I laughed at him and agreed I wouldn't. I showed him around the slightly disorganised space and told him where everything was, so if he wanted it, he could just get up and get it himself.

Since my secret was out and my darkness had been overpowered by light, I had been in my Art Cave several times. *I had won the war.* Being in there made me feel like my old self – just a better, stronger model. I removed my evidence pieces and stacked them in the corner. I covered them with a blanket. I was still deciding what I should do with them. A part of me wanted to start a bonfire and light them up. Watch them burn and become ash. Another part of me wanted to keep them – not to hang them in my room or look at them every day – but to have them there, just in case one day I had an art exhibit of my very own and I was brave enough to share them.

"So how is my tattoo art coming along? Any progress?" Kai said.

"I've sketched a few things but nothing's ready to show you. Right now I don't feel that they're good enough to be a permanent mark on your skin."

"They *must* be good then. Isn't this how you felt about the one Liam got done?"

"Kind of. It didn't start out as a tattoo though."

"Can I see one of your sketches? Pretty please."

"No." I smiled. "Not yet."

"Go on, just a glimpse."

"We'll see."

Once Kai became bored with his creation, he went over to the wall where my other canvases were stacked. He lifted up certain pieces and presented them to me, telling me which ones were his favourites, which ones he wished he had created and which ones he would take the credit for if he were speaking with art critics.

We spent the rest of the night in the lounge watching TV and talking. For a little while, Mum joined us. I leant back and relished the moment. I felt happy – true happiness.

A colour I never wanted to lose again.

Chapter THIRTY-SIX

My phone beeped and woke me. Groaning slightly, I rolled over and reached for it. It was a text from Kai.

Kai: Your presence is essential/required at the coffee shop. Be here in half an hour! OXOX
Me: Do I need to bring anything?
Kai: Just yourself.

I smiled.
My phone beeped again.

Kai: And maybe a kiss for me!

As I made my way to the coffee shop, I noticed how much the sun tried to shine through the thinning clouds. It was rare that I saw the sunrise. I couldn't help but feel joyful. The beaming orange and gold reached across the lower sky, making the lilac clouds look like fairy floss. The sunlight arced across the pavement and between the houses. A flock of birds patterned the distance in front of me and I felt as free as them.

The seasons were changing. Spring had started and I was ready for the newness it brought. Last night's rain and the morning sun created the rainbow that stretched across the sky. The colours linked and my eyes happily welcomed the beautiful sight. I felt like I had been living in grey for so long that I was seeing colours for the first time. We were being reintroduced, a colour at a time, and they fitted into my vision almost perfectly.

Kai's invitation was curious because I knew the coffee shop wasn't open for another hour. He was waiting outside, leant against the doorframe, dressed in his usual all-black uniform, his hair slicked back in a bun. I caught his attention and a wide smile stretched across his face.

"Good morning, Peyton Swift."

"Morning Kai."

He gently pulled me in. We kissed.

"What's going on? Is everything OK?"

"Everything's fine, Peyton. I have a surprise for you,"

"A *surprise*? What is it?"

"Well, if I told you before I showed you, then it wouldn't be a surprise anymore, would it?"

"Well where is this surprise? You know I don't ..."

"I know you're not the biggest fan of surprises, but doing surprises is sort of my thing; you'll learn to love them."

I stared at him and tried to uncover answers, but his face

gave nothing away. Nerves fluttered in my stomach. Not the bad kind, the beautiful kind taking flight – making me feel childish excitement.

"Are you ready?" Kai asked.

I took a deep breath. "I guess so."

"Close your eyes …"

"What? Is that necessary?"

"Closing your eyes is a *vital* part of this moment." He smiled.

"OK."

"Just close your eyes, take my hand and trust me."

I closed my eyes and held out my hand. Kai locked his fingers with mine.

"OK, I'm going to guide you. It's pretty simple; we'll be taking a few steps forward and I'm one thousand per cent sure you've walked through an open door before."

We started to move. The door opened. The usual sound of the bell rang overhead. He closed the door then let go of my hand.

"Keep your eyes closed."

My butterflies fluttered wildly. I couldn't erase my smile.

Kai stood behind me and whispered. "Open your eyes."

For a couple of seconds I kept them closed. I wanted to hold the unknown for a brief moment more. I took a breath in then opened my eyes.

I no longer felt my heart. My breath was taken from me. I stood in disbelief as I scanned the shop. My jaw dropped. "Kai … When did you? *How* did you?"

"Do you like it?"

"I ... I ..."

"Should I take that as a yes?"

I turned to Kai but I couldn't speak. My attention rushed back to two pieces of my artwork hanging on the coffee-shop walls. More of my canvases were spread out, leaning against the walls. Every piece of artwork was mine. "What is this?"

"Well, after you choose which works you want to hang up, it will be your own exhibition. Your *first* exhibition, if I'm not mistaken."

I felt undeserving. "Are these even *allowed* to be up here?"

"*Yeah* of course they are!"

I was stuck in amazement. Twisted with confusion. "How?"

"Must I reveal how I prepare *all* of my surprises?"

"Maybe. I don't know ... I'd *really* like to know for this one though."

"Well, I've had this idea for a while. One of the days when we were together in your Art Cave, I took photos of some of your art and then showed them to my boss. He loved them and said that if I could get the artist's permission we could hang them up the next time we changed the art."

"How did you sneak these out of the house? *When* did you sneak them out of the house?"

"Well, you can thank your mum for that."

"What?"

"I told her about my idea and she thought it was *great*, or did she say *amazing*? I think I recall the word *genius* being used." Kai laughed.

I shook my head.

"Anyway, last night your mum messaged me, letting me know you were in bed and we took the selected art from the cave, then this morning I hung a couple up and arranged the others around the room, then messaged you as soon as I could, hoping and praying that you wouldn't go into your Art Cave."

I was about to speak, but Kai interrupted.

"And before you say *anything*, I know you don't like people going in your cave unless you're there with them, but *this* was an important circumstance and ..."

"Kai. Shut up."

He took a breath.

"This is incredible. Thank you. Thank you *so* much." I kissed his cheek.

"Oh, I forgot to mention, like you already know, most or all of the art that we hang here is for sale, so, if you're up for it, you could sell yours."

I was still caught in surprise.

"Well, are you going to start setting up? Customers will be here before we know it."

"Um ... Yeah." I smiled.

"Just tell me what to do, Boss."

The early-morning customers arrived. I was there for a couple of hours, soaking up my first-ever art exhibition. I couldn't wait to call Liam and let him know. I knew I had to take pictures, maybe even a video. I knew he would be just as excited and happy as I was.

I was perched at a two-seater table near the counter so I could observe everything with an iced coffee in my hand. I felt like I was buzzing. I didn't even want to try to hide my excitement.

A mid-thirties couple strolled in. The girl wore her auburn hair in a knot on top of her head. Her short flimsy white dress was paired with brown boots and a jacket. Chunky rings overtook her fingers. Her partner wore a light-blue long-sleeve t-shirt paired with jeans and ankle boots. His black hair was tousled from his face. His beard looked like a shadow, making his blue eyes glisten.

"Wow. Babe, look at these …" The girl's wide eyes searched the walls like she was in a candy store. She stepped closer to one of my personal favourites. The face of a girl, wearing a flower crown with petals running down her flowing hair. Her eyes were straight ahead. Focused. Strong. She was made of only turquoise and purple. The effects of the watercolours dripping down the canvas drew your eyes up and down.

"Eddie, they're for sale …" She smiled. Her red lips made her teeth look whiter. "One of these would look *amazing* in our home. It would finish off the lounge perfectly. Don't you think?"

Eddie nodded.

"You know it would be an awesome statement piece and it would fit with how we've just decorated. Do you like it?"

"Yeah … Is this the one you'd want?"

"Well I mean I want to check out the others, but I *love* this one."

As his girlfriend continued looking at my art, Eddie went to the counter. I overheard him ask if he could put that piece on hold. I slapped my hand over my mouth. I couldn't stop my smile from growing.

Other customers' comments kept me beaming. This moment made me believe in myself and my art. Their words sparked fresh inspiration. I wanted to rush home and create something new. And I wouldn't have any limitations, because now I see the light. Now I see in colour.

ACKNOWLEDGEMENTS

Writing this novel has been such an adventure, one that I will treasure forever … Thank you for reading it.

The characters and the story fought their way (quite forcefully) to the keyboard and I'm so glad this story chose me. *Finding Technicolour* will always hold a dear place in my heart.

It feels peculiar writing acknowledgments, (but I'm so excited I've come this far!) I want to start with the largest possible thank you to everyone who's been involved (an umbrella thank you, just in case I forget to mention anyone in particular).

To all the ears I've bent discussing characters and plot points, thank you for your patience, honesty, advice, thoughts, ideas (the list goes on & on). Thank you from the bottom of my heart for believing in me & my words – and for filling my world with colour!

Everyone at A Story To Tell, thank you for letting me into your family and making me feel welcome as a new writer. To the wonderful Ann Bolch, thank you for believing in the story/stories that I have to tell. Your constant encouragement, kindness and wisdom have shaped me into the writer I am today. (I'll always love our handwritten letters).

Richard Holt, thank you for believing in me and for your honesty and guidance. This story wouldn't be what it is now without you.

I have mad respect for all the proof readers out there, so a big thank you to Heather Kelly for your fierce eye.

Aimee Coveney, thank you for my beautiful book cover – I can't picture it any other way. You're amazing!

Thank you to my family for their boundless love and support. You are all colours I feel safe in. Extra heartfelt thank you to my wonderful Mum, who read every draft. I always look forward to book clubbing with you!

My fabulous friends: Rhiannon Woolf, Holly Campbell, Jennifer Ibrahim, Laura Steen thank you for your unwavering support and belief in me and for being the marvellous people that you are.

Darcy Conroy … Where to begin? Thank you seems too simple a phrase. Your endless support, encouragement and insight throughout this entire process has been incredible and I am truly thankful. Having you in my corner and as a fellow writing buddy, means more to me than you'll ever know.

Thank you. Thank you. Thank you. XO_RR

ABOUT THE AUTHOR

Rebecca Rose lives in Melbourne, where she relishes in the stories whichever form they come – books, music, movies, TV shows.

Finding Technicolour is Rebecca's first novel.

Follow Rebecca on Instagram & Twitter @r_roseofficial or visit her website online at www.rebeccaroseofficial.com